TERROR IN D.C.

TERROR IN D.C.

RANDY WAYNE
WHITE
WRITING AS CARL RAMM

OPEN ROAD
INTEGRATED MEDIA
NEW YORK

Cover design by Andy Ross

ISBN: 978-1-5040-3521-7

This edition published in 2016 by Open Road Integrated Media, Inc.
180 Maiden Lane
New York, NY 10038
www.openroadmedia.com

TERROR
IN D.C.

ONE

At 4 A.M. three members of a terrorist organization planted bombs beneath the bedroom window and the kitchen window of Chester A. Rutledge's split-level home in Bethesda, Maryland.

It was a Friday morning, a school day, and at 6:30 A.M. Rutledge's sixteen-year-old son, Luke, was the first to awaken. He yawned, threw back the covers, and headed immediately for the bathroom in the hope of getting there before his thirteen-year-old sister, Mary Ann, his eleven-year-old sister, Lisa, and his four-year-old brother, Jeffery, whom everyone called J.R.

Mrs. Betty Rutledge was the next to awaken. As she passed the bathroom, she smiled sleepily at her oldest son and blew him a kiss. She wore a pale gray robe that made her blond hair look flaxen and her blue eyes glow.

"Ham or bacon, Luke?" she asked him.

"Both?"

His mother laughed. "Sure, why not. And what about the eggs?"

"Poached. Four of them."

"My little boy is growing up."

Luke Rutledge inspected his face for acne in the mirror. "I wish I could make Dad believe that."

"Oh, he believes it. He may be trying to postpone it a little, but he believes it. And, whether you think so or not, dear, your father only wants what's best for you."

The boy turned away from the mirror and looked carefully at his mother. "I guess I was out of line last night, huh? I should never have yelled at Dad like that. I should never have said those things. It's just that those three idiots in the Lincoln who hit us—"

"Everyone says things they don't mean when they're mad," his mother interrupted, not wishing to hear the story again.

"But I've never talked to him like that before. I'm kind of surprised he . . . he didn't smack me or something. Now I sorta wish he had."

His mother went to him and patted his head down onto her shoulder. "When you love someone, Luke, dear, words can hurt a lot worse than a slap."

"What I said was that bad?"

The boy's mother continued to pat his head. "I think what you said hurt him more deeply than you know—or you would never have said it. You and your father are a lot alike, Luke. Neither of you show much emotion, and that just makes it harder on both of you. But don't worry, dear—if you feel badly about it, just tell him when he gets up. Your father will understand . . . He cares for you so. I'm sure he'll forgive you."

The boy's eyes were suddenly glassy. "You really think so?"

Betty Rutledge was sure of it because she and her husband

had stayed up late worrying over the argument. Her husband's feelings *had* been badly hurt, but he wanted nothing so much as to regain his son's respect and affection. She did not tell her son that. Instead, she said, "I think you'll both feel much better if you have a good talk. Okay?"

"Yeah, Mom, sure. And thanks."

Her son was whistling as she walked through the dusky halls to the kitchen. She plugged in the automatic coffee maker, put a skillet on for the poached eggs, and began to make toast. Upstairs, she could hear the clump and giggle of her daughters waking up, and soon, she knew, she would hear the familiar sounds of toilets flushing, showers purling, hair dryers whining as her daughters went through their preschool routine.

Little J.R., hair mussed with sleep, thumb in his mouth, would be the last to come down, dragging his blanket behind.

This was Betty Rutledge's favorite time of day. She was alone with her thoughts, but she still had her family around her, warm and loving, with their troubles, their small triumphs. It was in the morning that the four kids and her husband, Chester, seemed exclusively hers; in the morning before school or sports or the office took them away into the world.

She poured herself a cup of coffee and began to prepare breakfast.

At 6:58 A.M. Luke came clomping into the kitchen. He piled bacon on top of a piece of toast and jammed half of it in his mouth.

His mother asked, "Do you have practice tonight?"

"Um-huh."

"It's Kevin's mother's turn to drive, isn't it?"

"Yup." He took another bite. "Wheremyeggs?"

"What? Was I supposed to understand that?"

The boy swallowed. "Where are my eggs?"

"They'll be done in about two minutes. Did you talk to your father?"

"He isn't out of bed yet. I guess he's sleeping in."

"Maybe you'll have to wait until after school to see him."

"Naw, I'd rather be late for class. I don't mind. I'm kind of anxious to talk to him. It's important."

Betty Rutledge remembered that it was after two when her husband finally shut off the bedroom light. She nodded her consent. "Then why don't you go outside and get his paper for him? The boy missed the sidewalk entirely this morning. I can see it lying out in the street."

"The kid's got no arm. When I had that route, I dented doors."

"And broke windows. Don't remind me. I remember the calls."

Laughing, Luke Rutledge walked through the dark living room and out the front door. It was a cool May morning, cherry-blossom time in Bethesda and nearby Washington, D.C. The sky was orange above the suburban houses across the street, and a cusp of moon tilted low in the west. The streetlights were still on.

The boy sidled into the street and picked up *The Washington Post*. He pulled it out of its tubular plastic bag and unfolded it. The lead story on the front page was about terrorists. They had been setting off bombs in Washington every week for the past six weeks. The terrorists seemed to bomb at random, striking civilian homes late at night or early in the morning. So far, six families had been murdered.

"Officials Fear Resumption of Bombings" was the headline.

Luke Rutledge had read about the bombings before, so he flipped through the first two sections to the sports page. He wanted to see how the Orioles were doing. Then for some reason, he found his eyes drawn to the house. His father stood at his bedroom window looking out at him. He wore no shirt and the hair on the broad chest was grayer than the thin hair on his head. Luke felt his face flush, embarrassed. But then his father's hand lifted in a tentative wave and he smiled a shy, boyish smile.

Suddenly feeling much better, Luke waved and smiled in return. The boy took a step toward the house, but the inside part of the paper fell onto the asphalt. He stooped to pick it up . . . and the world suddenly went white. His ears roared, his face burned, and there was a strange sensation of flying.

Then he was on his feet, walking in a daze. Someone stood beside him, pulling at his arm. It took Luke a long moment to recognize the man—Mr. Di Ornado, a neighbor from across the street. Mr. Di Ornado seemed to be shouting at him, but Luke could hear nothing because of the ringing in his ears. He noticed without emotion that several of the neighboring houses seemed to be on fire. But where was his house?

Luke jerked his arm away from Mr. Di Ornado and ran down the sidewalk toward a junkyard of smoldering bricks and lumber and burning furniture in the lawn where his home had once been.

His hands began to pull frantically at the debris as if they were being operated by a mind other than his own. This is weird, he thought. I'm looking through a trash pile, and I don't even know what I'm looking for. I'd better hurry, or I'll be late for school.

Then he saw something he recognized. The object was tubular, metallic, a scorched-blue. He pulled it out and looked at it blankly. It was a bicycle frame.

Somebody wrecked my ten-speed, he thought. Why would they do that?

Then he saw something else: a tiny hand attached to a smoldering pile of something that was wrapped in his little brother's Scooby-Doo pajamas. Several feet beyond, alone on a slab of board, his father's face peered at him quizzically. It was an odd expression, and Luke stared back at the face. Why aren't you smiling? he wondered. We're friends again, aren't we?

For long seconds, Luke stood frozen.

Then he dropped the bicycle frame, recoiling. He took a slow step back, then another. *"Daddy?"* he whispered hoarsely. *"Daddy!"*

Then he was running wildly, blindly down the street, swinging at the neighbors in their bedclothes as they tried to stop him.

During the seventeen months Luke Rutledge was to spend in George Washington University Hospital psychiatric center, he would speak no other word . . .

At 7:15 A.M. three students stepped from their dormitory out onto the campus of American University. The traffic on Nebraska Avenue and Foxhall Road was bumper-to-bumper.

To the southwest the Washington Monument was a pale funerary beneath the blue May haze. From the distance, sirens screamed.

The three students heard the sirens and paused to listen. One by one, they smiled and nudged each other.

"Aiee! It seems our mission was a success, brothers," said the leader, Mosul Aski. He looked at his expensive watch. "And right on time too."

"Should we be surprised? Once again, your plan was flawless, Mosul. We may have helped deliver the bombs, but it is you who deserves the praise! You are proving yourself an able leader to our elders in the homeland."

"Yes," laughed the third student, "but when the day comes for you to take your rightful seat as master of our people, do not forget your two old friends. Remember how I was injured in the service of the Motherland!"

The other two laughed with him. Because their leader, Mosul Aski, feared that the front and rear entrances of the dorm might be under surveillance, they had reentered the building early that morning by a window the American students used to sneak in women. Karaj, who was very fat, had gotten stuck in the window and had scraped his belly while being pulled through.

"I will not forget, Karaj." Mosul smiled. "But this day, let us not think of wounds. Let us rejoice! The cowardly American pig and his little piglet son are dead, and the American newspapers and television stations will again remind the world of our great cause. But before we celebrate, brothers, we have things to do. Zanjen, it is your turn to telephone *The Washing-*

ton Post with news of our victory. Remember—tell them only what I have told you to say. Do not give them time to trace the call, for they surely will try. Karaj, you must call Isfahan at the embassy. Isfahan, our honored leader, will be very happy. Be careful, though! Speak only of the kindness of our professors. That is the code for a successful mission. Now more than ever, we must be careful. Our necks are not the only ones on the block!"

"And what will you do, Mosul?"

"I have an eight o'clock appointment at the student loan office."

"But why?"

Mosul Aski, tall, slim, with a black mustache and a dark Mediterranean face, grinned with sarcasm. "If we are to retain our diplomatic scholarships for next year, there are forms that must be completed! Have you forgotten that it is the great and generous United States that pays for our education? Where is your gratitude, brothers!"

TWO

James Hawker swung shut the cylinder of his Colt .44-caliber stainless-steel revolver and stepped out into the street. It was a dirt street with a row of dingy houses on one side and a field of rank weed and junk on the other side.

To his right a door creaked open. Hawker raised the weapon in both hands, but stopped himself just as an old woman walked from a house carrying a shopping bag.

As Hawker lowered his revolver two men swung out from behind a clump of bushes. The guns in their hands looked like Lugers, only longer, less metallic, more space-aged. Hawker dove for his life and rolled hard as laser beams sizzled into the ground behind him.

He came up on one knee and fired twice, carefully. The skull of the first man exploded into small shards. The chest of his companion became a gaping black hole.

Once he was sure they were legitimate kills, Hawker got to his feet and continued down the street.

Overhead, through the camouflage mesh that covered the

area, a half-dozen 747s banked like vultures as they waited their turn to land at Washington's International Airport. From the far distance the sound of heavy traffic could be heard. The vigilante noticed neither the planes nor the traffic. His concentration was total.

Despite the cool wind that blew off the Potomac, Hawker wore only a thin black cotton crew-neck sweater, jeans, New Balance running shoes, and aluminum-tinted glasses. The wind mussed his short reddish-brown hair, but he did not feel the cold. He had come to this killing ground to prove himself, and nothing could draw his attention away from the job he had to do.

Ahead and to the left was a tanker truck. The fuel tank was made of stainless steel and brightly labeled DANGER! EXTREMELY FLAMMABLE! The truck was parked on a steep grade at the curb next to a building with a sign that read FORT STANTON PRESCHOOL AND NURSERY.

From within the building Hawker could hear the clear voices of children singing.

It presented an interesting problem. He suspected there were one or more of his adversaries waiting for him behind the truck. They could fire at him safely, but if he returned their fire he might ignite the tanker and take the lives of a hundred innocent children with him—and that was unthinkable. If it came to that, he would have to take the laser beams in the chest and be done with it.

Was there some way he could lure them safely away from the tanker? No, not these guys. Not a chance. He might as well try to get the moon to leave its orbit.

There might be one other safe way to do it . . .

Hawker moved toward the cover of the brush across the street. Then, without warning, he turned and sprinted toward the tanker truck. He caught a glimpse of two figures swinging out to meet him as his left foot touched the truck's steps and he dove through the open window into the cab. Even before he pulled his legs in behind him, Hawker released the emergency brake and knocked the gearshift into neutral. The hill was steep enough, and the truck began to roll.

Now sitting at the wheel, the vigilante let the truck coast for more than a block. Not trusting the air brakes without the engine running, he double-clutched and shifted into low to bring the huge rig to a stop. Before it stopped completely, though, he swung the door open and hit the street on the run. As he suspected, his adversaries had clung to the truck and made the ride with him. Hawker swung the Colt up in a two-handed grip. If he hit the tank now, no one would be killed but the killers—and maybe himself. He sighted carefully down the Jensen illuminated bead sights and squeezed the trigger twice.

The cannonlike impact of the .44 magnum severed the arm off one man, and tumbled the second man onto the ground.

Hawker snapped open the cylinder, ejected the four empties, reloaded, and trotted off down the street.

The next man waiting to kill him stood in an open third-floor window. Hawker glimpsed him from the corner of his eye, swung too quickly, and fired. Shots of unfamiliar elevation are always the toughest to make, and Hawker's clipped the man's shoulder. It would have knocked most men to the ground, but not this one. The laser gun beaded in on Hawker's heart as the vigilante hurried two more shots.

These did not miss.

The man tumbled from the window soundlessly.

Reloading on the run, Hawker was not prepared for what happened next. A block beyond the preschool, there was a strange *whuff* sound, followed by a deafening explosion, and just a few yards ahead of him where the smoke bomb landed, an acidic purple haze filled the air.

Immediately, Hawker dropped to his belly, gun poised. Coming at him through the fog were three tall figures. Hawker fought the urge to fire blindly, forcing himself to wait until he could make definite identification.

He was glad he did.

The first two were women dressed in white smocks, carrying black bags: doctors. Behind them, though, was a man with a gun held at their heads. The women were being held hostage. As Hawker knew, better than most, in any hostage situation the loss of one life usually motivates kidnappers to fire more freely.

In this operation blood had already been spilled.

Trying to use the purple fog to his advantage, Hawker lay motionless until the last possible moment. The women doctors stood not quite shoulder to shoulder. The man stood between them.

There was plenty of room for a safe shot, and Hawker took it, taking slow, careful aim.

The killer's head exploded from his shoulders as the two doctors dropped to the ground.

The vigilante stood and looked at the two women. "You could at least say thanks," he said wryly.

The women lay motionless, saying nothing.

Hawker moved on.

His objective was the brick house at the end of the street. There, he would be safe.

But he still had a long fifty yards to go.

Hawker walked quickly, then began to trot. He was anxious to get this battle over with, and the only way to do it was to force the opposition into the open. To kill him, they had to show themselves.

It didn't take long for them to appear.

A lone gunman swung to meet him from behind a high white fence. The vigilante's hurried shot was low, just above the groin. But with a Colt .44, any placement in the trunk area is a man-stopper.

The figure collapsed on the ground.

He had only twenty yards to go now. Did he really have a chance of making it? Maybe. But he couldn't allow himself to think about it. Any lapse of attention in this business could mean death.

Hawker continued to jog, head swiveling, gun ready.

Then the brick house was only ten yards away, then five . . . and then he knew he would make it. But just as he was about to step onto the porch of the brick house, three big men jumped up from behind the white fence at once. Hawker caught his breath in surprise while the big Colt began to blaze in his hands.

Hawker took the man in the middle first, dove and rolled,

then cut down the man closest to him, then the man on the far left.

The sudden silence was eerie. They were dead. All of them, dead.

Hawker got to his feet breathing heavily. How many rounds had he used? Four, maybe five? He had at least one left, but it didn't matter. He had made it.

He swung open the gate to the brick house and stepped up onto the porch. Just as he was about to reach for the door-knob, the door slammed open. Hawker drew up the Colt, but stopped just in time.

It was another woman carrying a bag of groceries.

"Don't the ladies in this town have anything better to do than shop?" Hawker smiled as he moved to step by her.

As he did, the woman dropped the grocery bag. Hawker watched in disbelief as a gun materialized in her hand far too quickly for him to react.

The woman shot him once, in the left side of the chest.

James Hawker backpedaled into the railing and somer-saulted backward into the street, thinking of nothing but the terrible pain in his heart . . .

THREE

"You're dead, Hawker. Too bad. So tell me, is there really a heaven? Or just a hell?"

James Hawker opened his eyes slowly. Looming above him was a tall, lanky man with thin blond hair and a craggy, Wisconsin smile. He wore a black tie, a baggy gray suit, and a white shirt.

The vigilante got slowly to his Feet, his breath whistling through his teeth at the electric pain that still Ping-Ponged between his brain and his toes.

"Jesus Christ, Rehfuss." He grimaced. "You told me getting shot by one of those laser beams hurt, but you didn't say it was like getting hit by a flame thrower."

Lester Rehfuss, department director of the Central Intelligence Agency's Small Arms Training Division, added a patronizing flair as he brushed the dust from Hawker's sweater. "I told you we'd made it as close to an actual firefight situation as possible, and that means a man has to pay dearly for any mistakes he makes. Let's face it, Hawker, you made a mistake. Never trust old ladies with shopping bags."

Hawker ripped the aluminum-tinted goggles from his face in disgust. The goggles protected his eyes from the low-intensity laser beams the computer-controlled mannequins fired. "Damn it," he said, "I almost made it."

The smile left the CIA man's face. "*Almost* made it? Is that supposed to impress me? The last time the CIA *almost* made it, we got our asses chewed good for printing a little manual in Spanish that had the audacity to tell Nicaraguan rebels how to eliminate the Commie goons who have taken over their country. You still don't get it, do you, Hawker? In this business, we can't afford even the tiniest mistake. 'Almost' isn't good enough—not because of what our enemies will do, but because of how our own news media will tear us to bits. Every time we screw up, the Dan Rathers and the Barbara Walters scream and whine and condemn until the Congress is forced to pull our leash just a little tighter. And if it gets much tighter, friend, we might as well trade our badges in for Boy Scout manuals."

Hawker held his chest and rolled his head experimentally. "I don't doubt it, Lester, but I'm in no mood for lectures. Besides, I'm out of the picture now. You people invited me in to give me a . . . what did you call it? Yeah, a screen test. Well, I just blew the screen test. So, if you don't mind, I'll just turn in my temporary security pass and head on back to my hotel. I think maybe soaking in a hot tub for three or four hours may make me feel well enough to get on a plane back to Florida."

"Just like that? What about the people who pulled so many strings to get you this far?"

"You said it was a pass-or-fail test."

"That's right."

"And one of your motorized hit ladies has just turned me into a statistic. A clean kill if I ever saw one."

"Nice back somersault you did too. Were you ever a gymnast?"

"Just full of jokes, aren't you?" Hawker began to dust off his jeans, then stopped suddenly. "Hey, wait a minute—why are you stalling? You don't have to kill me now, do you? I mean, I came in here to your secret training installation and you showed me around, but now I've messed up the routine by failing your little test. What do you people do with outsiders who've seen too much?"

"Aside from poke their eyes out with hot sticks, you mean?"

"Come on, Lester, it's a legitimate question."

"Then I'll give you a legitimate answer—but let's wait until after your evaluation."

Hawker looked at him with suspicion. "Why is it this is the first I've heard of any kind of evaluation?"

Lester Rehfuss smiled. "Don't you read the papers? It's because the CIA is just plain sneaky."

Hawker shrugged and picked up the Colt .44, which lay several yards away where it had landed in the dirt. He clicked open the cylinder and began to eject the live round before he stopped and smiled wryly at Rehfuss. "Maybe I shouldn't unload this thing?"

"Do what you want, James. But slapping a loaded revolver down on the table isn't going to make the man chairing your evaluation look any more kindly on you."

"Oh? And who's that?"

The smile faded from Rehfuss's face. "Admiral Percival, my boss."

"Admiral?"

"Unless you're one of the two or three people in this whole world he actually likes, then he's *Max* Percival. But you don't have to worry about that, James. The admiral isn't going to like you. He isn't going to like you one little bit . . ."

Hawker followed Lester Rehfuss back down the dirt street, past the movie-set house facades and past the empty tanker truck. Children's voices no longer floated from the nursery school—the reel-to-reel tape inside had been switched off. Up and down the street, CIA technicians were already busy replacing the plastic heads and trunks of the mannequins Hawker had "killed." The mannequins were fixed on steel tracks for mobility, and thick black cables ran from their laser guns to an unseen source of power.

The vigilante rubbed his chest thoughtfully. The firefight test had been lifelike, all right. He hoped he was never asked to try it again.

The complex was located on the south side of Washington, D.C., not far from Bolling Air Force Base and the Naval Research Lab. Its entire ten acres was encircled by high military fencing, and camouflage netting covered the open areas. James Hawker had come here every day for the last three days. He had been interviewed by a dozen men whose last names he never knew. He had been asked searching questions by men in white smocks who he assumed were psychiatrists. He had been given a bank of written tests far more demanding than any he had ever taken in college or at the police academy in Chicago.

And why?

Because his friend and associate, Jacob Montgomery Hayes, one of the wealthiest men in the world, had sent a messenger to Hawker's newly acquired fish shack on the west coast of Florida asking him to fly to Washington, D.C., immediately.

No explanations were offered. And, from Hayes—a man Hawker respected and admired—none were required.

Hawker caught the first flight from Miami to Washington International.

Lester Rehfuss met him at the airport, showed him to his hotel, and finally gave him a short briefing on the terrorist bombings. That was on a Monday. Rehfuss told him that seven civilian houses, apparently at random, had been bombed by a person or persons unknown. Because the bombing of the Rutledge home was the most recent—it had occurred only three days before—Rehfuss went into greater detail about it. So far, twenty-seven innocent, unsuspecting men, women, and children had been murdered.

The only survivor was Luke Rutledge, age sixteen, and he was now catatonic, so psychologically disturbed that he could not speak.

Hawker tried to pry more information out of Rehfuss. Had he been ordered to Washington to help? Who was behind it? How could anyone be sure the bombings were random? Didn't there have to be some pattern behind it?

Rehfuss refused to answer. All he told Hawker was that he

might be able to help, but first they had to be sure he was capable. Would Hawker submit to any tests asked of him?

Hawker consented on the spot.

It wasn't until the next day he learned that Lester Rehfuss was with the CIA.

Hawker followed Rehfuss out of the firefight test area past a line of big corrugated steel and brick buildings. The doors on all of them warned ABSOLUTELY NO ADMITTANCE WITHOUT CLEARANCE!

Each door was guarded by a brace of Marines in battle dress.

For the first time Hawker realized he had actually seen very little of the complex in his three days there.

He wondered why he was being allowed to see more.

A modern paved street ran along the stretch of buildings, but the only vehicles there were either jeeps or unmarked government cars in bland colors.

Rehfuss stopped at a white-brick three-story house that looked like the solid old residence of a small-town doctor.

"This is it," he said.

"Shouldn't I change clothes? Wash up? Practice my Morse code?"

"Smart ass." He tossed Hawker the sport jacket he had been carrying for him. "Put this on—at least try to cover up that cannon you've got strapped under your arm. Like I said, the admiral isn't going to like you much as it is."

Two Marines challenged their approach. Hawker had become used to the extreme security measures. They studied his Pliofilmed ID carefully, then they watched as first Rehfuss, then Hawker, touched their thumbs to the photoelectric eye after first inserting their IDs into the gray steel box beside the entrance.

The computers would match their thumb prints against those on the IDs and those in the computer's files.

Almost immediately the doors swung open. The Marines did a salute arms as they went inside.

Hawker had never been inside the building before. Unlike most of the office complexes, this one lacked the stark military atmosphere of gray steel desks and bare linoleum floors. There was carpeting and soft neon lighting. In each office vestibule serious-looking women wearing ID badges worked at desktop computers.

"So where are we headed, oh, leader?" Hawker asked.

Rehfuss stopped at the elevator and touched the button. "Do you like movies?"

"What kind of movies?"

"New movies."

Hawker shook his head. "Impossible. They stopped making movies when Cary Grant and John Wayne and David Niven left the business. Now they just make long TV programs. The male actors all go to the same hairstylist, and the female performers confuse bitchiness with acting. And if you can't tell, no, I don't like them."

"Don't speak too quickly. We have one today you may like."

"Does it have a happy ending?"

"Almost."

"Then don't expect a glowing review."

Still another Marine ushered them into a darkened room where a cement floor sloped toward a screen the size of a picture window: a movie room. The seating area was small, though, only about twenty plush chairs. Between the seating area and the screen the floor flattened abruptly, and there was a large table.

From the back of the room Hawker could see that five people sat in the front row. He couldn't see their faces.

Rehfuss took a seat midway down, and Hawker sat beside him. "Trying to humor me before I get my evaluation?"

"If I were trying to humor you, I'd have brought popcorn," Rehfuss said wryly. "Shut up and watch."

From the front row an older man with white hair and an anvil jaw turned slightly. "Is the applicant with you, Agent Rehfuss?"

"He is, Admiral."

In a louder voice, the admiral said, "Roll the film, then."

Without any sign of a projector being switched on, the screen was suddenly illuminated. Hawker was surprised to see himself standing in the dirt street of the firefight range, just closing the cylinder of his Colt .44 magnum. On the right side of the screen digits measuring minutes, seconds, and hundredths of seconds timed him.

The film was in color.

James Hawker settled back and watched with interest. Why not? This would be like being favored with a preview of the way he knew he would someday die . . .

FOUR

"I thought good guys always wore white," Rehfuss whispered with a smirk.

Hawker considered the screen and the black sweater he wore. "They do. Is that why all CIA agents wear gray suits?"

"*Touché.*"

"*Touché* yourself. How in the hell did your people get this thing processed and set up so fast?"

"It's on tape, for one thing. We used three department cameramen. They were inside the houses. And, believe it or not, it's not the first time we've ever tested someone. All the agents with a Blue Light rating get the firefight treatment."

"Blue Light rating?"

"When a person is shot in the head, supposedly all he sees is a blue light."

"Very romantic. Is that like a license to kill?"

"You read too many books. Watch yourself get outsmarted. Maybe you'll learn something."

So Hawker watched:

. . . watched as he nearly gunned down the mechanical lady with the shopping bag.

. . . watched as he blew away the two guys who jumped out of the bushes.

. . . watched as he dove into the tanker truck, got it rolling, then jumped out and nailed two more of the mannequins.

. . . watched as he wounded, then killed, the gunman in the third-floor window.

. . . watched all the rest of it, from the detonation of the smoke bomb to the final shoot-out with the three manne-quins on the porch and, finally, his own demise at the hands of the pistol-packing bag lady. As he watched, the memory of the searing pain he had felt made his muscles knot once again, but he didn't have long to think about it.

The lights went on almost immediately.

CIA Agent Lester Rehfuss was grinning. "Next time, get yourself a decent leading lady, Hawk. That mug of yours won't sell a single ticket."

"You were right about that back somersault I did. Pretty impressive."

"Got a pretty good laugh from a couple of the guys up front. Or didn't you notice?"

"Yeah, I noticed. And I'm just wondering how much it would cost me to buy a ticket to see them get hit by that god-damned laser beam."

"You really would like that?"

"Hell, they laughed, didn't they . . .?" But then Hawker saw what Rehfuss meant. The five people in the front row were on their feet now. Two of them turned and peered toward the rear of the theater as their eyes adjusted to the light.

Hawker had no trouble recognizing either of them.

The stocky, middle-sized man with the wire-rimmed glasses and the ascetic expression was Hawker's friend, Jacob Montgomery Hayes.

The other was tall, lean, saber-faced Hendricks, Hayes's acerbic butler.

Hawker hadn't seen either of them for more than five months, so he had to restrain himself as he approached them. They, too, seemed happy to see him, and they met him half-way up the aisle, away from the others.

"Christ, Jake," Hawker smiled, half whispering, "I knew you had connections, but I had no idea you were involved with the Central Intelligence Agency."

Hayes, in his mid-sixties, wearing an Irish tweed jacket and no tie, smiled in return. "I'm not involved with them, James. But a friend of mine got in touch with me last Saturday about this bombing business, and I had to pull a few strings. The strings led me here."

Hawker looked at the butler and grinned. "And Hank came along with you, too, huh?"

Hendricks hated to be called "Hank."

The butler lifted his eyebrows, which was about as close as he ever came to smiling. "Quite a performance you gave for the cameras, James," he said. "You die beautifully."

Hawker shook his head. "I'm sorry about that, guys. I really am. I wanted to help, and I took all their damn tests. And the one I thought I'd be best at, the firefight, is the one I failed."

"Would you gentlemen care to sit at the table while we go over a few things?" a voice called. It wasn't a question. It was an order. Admiral Maxwell Percival stood at the head of the long mahogany table addressing them. He wore a dark blue civilian suit. His hair was thick, pure white, and he had wild, bushy eyebrows.

"Be right with you, Max," Hendricks called back.

"*Max?*" Hawker asked.

"And what else would I call an American who was one of my subordinates in MI-5 during the war?" the Englishman asked with aplomb.

"Now you know one of the strings I had to pull," Jake Hayes whispered as the three of them, followed by Rehfuss, took their seats.

Only Admiral Percival remained standing. He began, "I need not remind you, gentlemen, that what is said here falls under the National Security Secrets Act of 1942. You may not repeat to anyone what is said here under penalty of law. To my left is Agent Miller, to my right is Agent Nelson. Agent Rehfuss is sitting next to the participant. These agents have been asked to evaluate the test results of the participant. Prior tests concerning intellectual, psychological, and physical fitness were all satisfactory. I will not go into those, nor will they be available for the participant's—or anyone else's—perusal. We are here solely to discuss the participant's performance on the firefight range. Agent Miller, you will give the first critique." In a louder voice, Admiral Percival said, "Please roll the film again."

Once more Hawker sat and watched as he ran the laser

gauntlet. Twice Agent Miller had the tape stopped to criticize Hawker's performance: for sloppy shooting when he only wounded the third-floor gunman ("Prone position is the most effective position for difficult shots"), and for reloading on the run ("He should have taken cover to reload. The participant had no idea where his adversaries were positioned").

When the film was over the lights came on once more. Admiral Percival did not stand. He nodded at the man to his left. "You are excused, Agent Miller."

When the door was closed the admiral once again asked for the tape to be shown, and Hawker sat silently while Agent Nelson offered criticism. He, too, had the film stopped twice. "When he was confronted by three adversaries at once, he shot the man in the middle first, then he shot the man to his right. He should have taken the man to his right first. The man was left-handed. Statistically, left-handed men are better marksmen. When he was confronted by the woman with the shopping bag who ultimately shot him, he should have known immediately she was an adversary. No woman would come out of a house only moments after three men had been shot on her porch. Her intent should have been clear to the participant."

Hawker said nothing, trying hard not to look like the idiot he felt himself to be. The CIA man was absolutely right—he should have known!

Agent Nelson was dismissed as perfunctorily as Agent Miller.

When he was gone Admiral Percival rubbed his forehead for a moment as if he had a slight headache, then looked up. "Agent Rehfuss, your summary?"

The craggy man with the thin blond hair cleared his throat. "Well, I thought Mr. Hawk—the participant—performed quite well. Extremely well, as a matter of fact. Perhaps I should remind the Admiral that only one agent in the three-year history of the firefight course has made it satisfactorily as far—"

"I'm familiar with past scores on the course," Percival cut in. "Please confine your summary to the matter at hand."

"I was about to say that the most common mistake is to assault the course without proper regard for civilian lives. Fifty-eight percent of the participants kill the first woman with the shopping bag. Seventy-six percent of the participants blow up the children in the preschool. Nineteen percent are killed trying to skirt the tanker truck and avoid a confrontation. Only five percent handle the situation satisfactorily, and only one other participant has scored kills on the tank-truck gunmen—"

"Your point has been made," the admiral said impatiently. "Please get on with your summary."

"That is my summary, Admiral. I thought the participant performed as well or better than anyone who has ever been through the course—and he did it without any training from us."

The admiral slammed his hand down on the table. "He was killed, damn it!"

"Yes, by a woman with a shopping bag."

"How can you not agree with Agent Nelson? He should have known her intentions from the moment he saw her!"

"It was undoubtedly a mistake."

"And a damn stupid mistake at that!"

"Quite stupid, sir." (Hawker winced.) "The participant obviously wasn't thinking clearly. He should have known, yes."

"And yet you insist his performance was good? Despite the sloppy shooting, despite his errors in judgment, despite the fact that he was killed?"

"I still feel his performance on the course was exceptionally good. As I said, only one other participant has ever done as well—"

"That's quite enough," grumped the admiral. "Thank you, Agent Rehfuss, for your summary."

Admiral Maxwell Percival folded his hands and cleared his throat, about to make a summation of his own. He nodded toward Hawker. "I cannot agree with the assessment of Agent Rehfuss. I do not think your performance was exceptional. It was, I feel, quite ordinary. In certain obvious ways, it was totally unsatisfactory. Please don't misunderstand my words. This is not a personal attack on you. My agency was asked to consider you for temporary assignment. The individuals making the request were people of such impeccable judgment that I could not, in good conscience, refuse to give you a trial. You have now had that trial and, in my judgment, did not complete it satisfactorily. The work of the Central Intelligence Agency is complex and sometimes dangerous. It is not work for amateurs, however good their intentions. We thank you for your concern."

Admiral Percival closed the folder on his desk and looked around the table. "Any comments?"

Hendricks was the first to speak. "I'm afraid I have to agree with you, Max. Awfully kind of you to let us have a fling, though."

"I should apologize for wasting so much of your time," Jacob Hayes put in. "We didn't realize the scope of the job involved when we first made the proposal."

Hawker couldn't believe his ears. He opened his mouth to speak, but Lester Rehfuss touched him on the shoulder and shook his head wordlessly.

Percival stood, shoved the folder under his arm, and headed for the door. As he passed Hawker, a slip of paper floated down on the table in front of him. The admiral seemed not to notice. "Good day, gentlemen," he called over his shoulder. "Have a safe journey home."

Hawker picked up the slip of paper that had fallen from the admiral's folder. There was writing on it. It read, Meet me for lunch at the Eastern Chalice in 30 minutes.

Hawker looked at Rehfuss. "This isn't for me, is it—"

"Thanks a lot for coming, gentlemen," the agent said loudly while giving Hawker a pointed look.

Obviously, he didn't want Hawker to acknowledge the note. Jake Hayes and Hendricks, he noticed, didn't look the least bit confused.

What the hell could it mean? Could somebody be eavesdropping? There were certainly people in the film room, but so what? This was the CIA, where everyone had maximum security clearance.

Why couldn't they speak openly?

Hawker shrugged. "Thanks for the chance, Lester," he said, shaking Rehfuss's hand.

"Our pleasure. I still think you looked pretty good out there, but the admiral knows more about it than I do—maybe that's why he has final say. I'll have the guards escort you to the compound exit."

"Lester," Hawker put in quickly, "there's one more thing I wanted to ask. You said one other man had done as well as I did on the course. Why in the hell don't you get him for this assignment?"

Rehfuss looked surprised for a moment, then smiled. "We'd love to, Mr. Hawker, we really would. Your styles are very much alike. *Very* much alike. Unfortunately, he was killed in the line of duty several months ago."

"Rehfuss," Hawker said dryly, "you really know how to boost a man's confidence."

FIVE

Half an hour later the lanky CIA man was waiting at a dark-ened table in the far corner of the Eastern Chalice Restaurant with Admiral Max Percival.

The Eastern Chalice was a Syrian ethnic hole-in-the-wall eatery on a street lined with go-go-dancer bars and massage parlors, just off the Anacostia River.

Hawker entered first, followed by Hayes and Hendricks. The Eastern Chalice had a chrome and glass dime-store facade, but inside it was dark and cool, and the air was spiced with incense. Beaded curtains covered the inner doorways, and the floors and walls were decorated with heavy Persian carpets. Hawker couldn't tell if the sitar music was from a radio or a tape.

The host wore a turban. He showed them to Percival's table and bowed a retreat after Rehfuss stuck a bill in his hand.

The admiral stood at their arrival, more cordial than he had been all morning. He thrust out his hand. "Hendricks, it's good to see you—still feel as if I ought to snap off a salute when I see you coming. Mr. Hayes, have a seat. I had one of

my people check, like you asked, and they do have vegetar-
ian dishes here. Mr. Hawker, no more criticism and no more
films—I promise."

The table was only knee-high, and Hawker sat on a satin
pillow between Rehfuss and Admiral Percival. "That's a relief,"
he said. "Back at the compound, I was beginning to feel like a
kid with braces applying to Harvard."

"The criticism from my two agents, you mean? I'm afraid
their points were absolutely valid."

Hawker nodded. "I hate to admit it, but I think they were
right, too, Admiral. That's what bothers me."

"Oh?"

"Yeah, I can't figure out why you have me here."

"Don't worry, Hawk." Rehfuss laughed. "The reasons aren't
all that obvious."

"Then tell me—"

"Gentlemen," Hendricks interrupted, "I suggest we order
first, then let Admiral Percival explain this meeting to James.
Does that seem sensible to you, Admiral?"

"You know damn well it does, Hank." The old Navy man
looked at Hawker. "See, like all good undercover men, Hank
has a real aversion to waiters flitting around. He wants to get
their business out of the way before he gets to his own."

"Exactly, sir."

The admiral laughed. "Would you believe that it was me
who used to call Hendricks 'sir'?"

"Believe it?" Jacob Hayes smiled. "He's my butler, and I *still*
find myself slipping up and calling him 'sir.' He gets a big kick
out of it."

Hawker ordered curried goat, brown rice, sour cream, black bread, and green tea. The men made small talk until the meal was finished, the plates cleared, and the dessert refused.

Over espresso in eggshell-thin demitasses, Admiral Percival began to speak. Unlike the earlier meeting, he spoke softly, reflectively, almost as if he were reminding himself why the five of them now sat at the same table.

He said, "Mr. Hawker, you've waited long enough for an explanation. The fact is, I want you to work for us. I was impressed by your performance on the firefight range, as well as the scores on your other tests. I am confident that you will conduct yourself with the best interests of this country, the agency, and the civilian population." The older man reached his hand across the table. "Still interested?"

After hesitating in surprise, Hawker shook his hand. "But why the brush-off back at the complex? I don't get it, Admiral. Everyone went along with you so easily—was I the only one not in on the joke?"

"Let's hope not," Hendricks said mildly. "The admiral wants no one—absolutely no one aside from us—to know you have been retained by the agency. That is why you were officially refused employment. As far as everyone involved with the CIA is concerned, you were considered for a special assignment, then turned away."

"But the fact is, James, we need a man just like you," the admiral continued. "I need someone who is as good as the best our Blue Light sector has to offer—but isn't connected with the CIA in any way. Let me explain from the beginning. Seven weeks and six days ago, a terrorist organization began to bomb civilian homes in the D.C. area. They have bombed one home a week since then, always on a Friday, Saturday, or Sunday night or early morning. The explosions are of such force that there has been only one survivor—a teenage boy who was not in his house at the time. On the morning following every bombing, someone—always a different male voice with an Arabic accent—calls *The Washington Post* and delivers the same message—'Another American family has been punished for the crimes of the United States against the peace-loving peoples of the Middle East.'

"Psychologically, the bombings are horribly effective. The weekly occurrence, the impossibility of knowing where the terrorists are going to strike next, have pushed the population near panic. Our agency, at the request of the President, has joined with the FBI and the city police to coordinate a massive investigation. But I'm sure you know how time-consuming a proper investigation is—and we still have all too little to go on. Victims do, indeed, seem to be chosen randomly. Protestants, Jews, Catholics, whites, and blacks have all been victims—twenty-seven, in all."

Hawker interrupted. "What about political affiliations? Any connections there?"

Percival shook his head. "All the victims were relatively conservative—which is to be expected from people with families. But they were a fairly even mix of Democrats and Republicans, with a few registered Independents."

"Did any of them work for our government?"

"Not in any major capacity."

"Did any of them have links to high-ranking government officials?"

"Only one. Last Friday the Chester Rutledge home in

Bethesda was bombed. Mrs. Betty Rutledge—the late Mrs. Rutledge—was the sister of Senator Thy Estes, a member of the Senate Foreign Relations Committee, and one of the most respected women on the Hill."

"Thy?"

"Yes. It's spelled T-H-Y, but it's pronounced like the first syllable of theater. She's quite a woman."

Jake Hayes spoke. "Remember I said a friend called me on Saturday and asked for my help? The friend was Senator Estes. She was still a little in shock, and terribly distraught. I've known the senator for many years and she knew, of course, how my own son was murdered by a terrorist. I think she called seeking comfort, but during the conversation I mentioned there might be a route more direct than the legal process to stop these madmen. She jumped at the idea, I knew something of your record as the founder of the Chicago SWAT team, James, so I immediately got in touch with you—"

"Mr. Hayes," Admiral Percival interrupted uneasily, "I'd rather not hear any more about your relationship with Mr. Hawker. I could tell you of the rumors my agency has heard about an auburn-haired American vigilante who, with an apparently inexhaustible source of financial backing, has declared war on the violent criminals of this nation. I could tell you, but I won't." The old Navy man smiled slightly. "In other words, you need not waste your time trying to disguise your relationship with Mr. Hawker. All I know is that Senator Estes recommended Mr. Hawker to my attention as a source of possible aid in a very difficult case. His services were refused—and that is all I care to know."

*　　*　　*

Hayes nodded his understanding. "Of course, Admiral. I was just explaining to James how he happened to be sitting here digesting goat instead of relaxing in Florida fishing for tarpon."

"And now that I'm here," Hawker put in, "I'm anxious to find out what you want me to do."

"Of course. As I was saying, the investigation has not been easy, but we have come up with a few tentative conclusions. The bombs they use are devastating. From the on-site debris, we know they are highly sophisticated devices. They are probably imported in their component parts and assembled here. Because of the frequency of the bombings, there's probably a permanent storage area for the materials. They may also be assembled at that site, but it is more likely that they do it elsewhere. We suspect the terrorists have tried to decentralize their operation as much as possible.

"Our investigators have hypothesized that on the morning of that night's attack, the terrorists leave their headquarters, go to the storage area for a single bomb's components, then take it to an assembly area for final construction. To have evaded our investigations so successfully, we must also assume that their storage and assembly areas enjoy very good security—a security so complete that they are beyond the normal jurisdiction of law-enforcement agencies. It's the only thing that makes sense."

"Yet the areas have to be in Washington, D.C.—or very nearby," Hawker said thoughtfully.

"Exactly."

"Then you have to suspect the obvious—that the terrorists are operating out of one or more of the foreign embassies."

Admiral Percival nodded emphatically. "We do suspect it. We strongly suspect it. We have tendered letters of inquiry to the embassies of all the Mideastern nations. Of course, their ambassadors show great indignation at even being questioned. They naturally disavow any knowledge of the bombings."

Hendricks added, "And, of course, the confines of all embassies are sacred ground—in this country, anyway. To violate their boundaries is to forfeit the sanctity of your own embassies all around the world."

"Not that they haven't been violated often enough," Percival added. "But Hank is right. If we forced an investigation on any of the embassies, it would be an international incident that would pretty much end the foreign embassy system. The President agrees. We can snoop all we want from the outside, but no one with any government connection can set foot inside."

It was suddenly clear to Hawker why he had been called to Washington. "And what would you do if you could send your people in?"

"My official agents? I would probably make sure they tiptoed around until they sniffed out the terrorists. I hate to think of the legalities involved. Embassy officials enjoy diplomatic immunity, you know. They can do anything, steal, rape, murder—and they have, more than once. And they can commit those crimes without fear of prosecution. Government spokesmen would probably call for their heads, give the newspapers exactly what they wanted to hear. In private, the government would be more likely to tell the bombers to get the hell out of the country and not to come back."

"And what if you had the use of an agent who was in no way connected with the CIA or the government?"

Admiral Maxwell Percival's sea-gray eyes became steely, and for the first time Hawker knew what kind of naval commander he must have been. "If I had such a man at my command, I would tell him to find out who was responsible. And once he was sure, sure beyond any shadow of a doubt, I would tell him to start lopping off heads and not stop until they were all dead. They've murdered twenty-seven innocent men, women, and children, James. Last week, they killed a four-year-old boy, his two sisters, and his parents. They're not people, they're insane animals. And they're due to strike again this weekend. They must be stopped. But if I had such an agent, I would warn him that he would be in the field alone. We would help him with information when we got it, but if he took a fall, if he got caught by any agency—including my own—he would spend a lot of lonely years in prison. This person would have to be a vigilante acting alone. But I would also tell him that there is a very good chance he might discover a very handsome chunk of money waiting for him if the mission was a success—a half-million dollars, say, in untraceable bills." The admiral thought for a moment. "In your case, though—"

"In my case, you were about to say, I am already a wealthy man." Hawker pushed his espresso away and poured himself more green tea. "Your people have no doubt read every record ever kept on me since kindergarten, so you know that I own part of a thriving oil business in Texas"—remembering the way little Sancho Rigera had stumbled into an oil bonanza during his Houston attack, Hawker grinned and looked at Hayes— "through no enterprise of my own, I might add. You're right, I don't need the money. But I imagine that whoever took this job would feel entitled to some sort of reward, and the figure you mentioned seems sufficient."

"You want it?"

"I already know how to spend it."

"Upon successful completion of your mission, of course."

"Right."

"Then it will be arranged."

"Admiral, I'm sure you have some specific embassies in mind. Have you narrowed it down at all?"

Percival made a gesture of uncertainty. "It could be any of them—or all of them. Frankly, I don't trust the diplomats from any of those countries. Most of them have been educated in Europe, or here, and they speak with charm and intelligence. But when you look at the very roots of the Arabic race, their history, their traditions, you see those people for what they are—desert nomads who care little for human life, and who have contributed almost nothing to world society. Were it not for their oil, they would be among the starving millions who simply cannot fend for themselves. Syria, Lebanon, Iraq, Iran—"

"But Iran has no embassy here, does it?"

"What? Yes . . . in a way. All countries, no matter what our relationship with them, keep some kind of staff here. A little over a year ago, with the help of certain American banks to whom the Iranians are heavily in debt, the Iranians were allowed to set up a sort of 'embassy in exile.' It is staffed by Iranians, Iranian-Americans, and a few Iranian students who work mostly as liaisons between the banks and their country. Even though it is an embassy in exile, they still enjoy diplomatic privilege. They keep offices at the World Exchange Bank, downtown. We have the offices under surveillance, and we've put taps on their communications lines. So far, though, we haven't come up with a thing."

"Wouldn't they be the most likely candidates for the bombings?"

"More likely than the Syrians or the Iraqis or the Lebanese? They all hate us. Who can say?" The admiral stood abruptly and, at some unseen signal, so did Rehfuss, Hendricks, and Jacob Hayes. They were leaving, and Hawker realized they intended to leave without him. The admiral continued, "If I really did have a free-lance agent, I would tell him there are all kinds of methods for getting information not available to us. And I would tell him he might be wise in starting with the man who owns this restaurant, a Syrian who, like many expatriates here, is a soldier in exile. His name is Rultan, and he has access to a great deal of information on the underground activities of the Mideastern countries." The admiral dropped a heavy manila envelope on the table. "Here, you may need this. These people understand two things—violence and money. Always try the money first. Now that you're on your own, it may be the best advice I can give you."

SIX

Hawker signaled for the waiter, a thin swarthy man with a walrus mustache and a turban.

"Your lunch was satisfactory, sir?"

Hawker nudged the bill tray toward him. The twenty and the five on the tray covered the bill, plus a standard tip. Hawker had another twenty hidden in his hand. He said, "The lunch was fine. Excellent, in fact. The curried goat was so good, I'd like to get the recipe. I was told a gentleman named Rultan could provide me with it."

"Mr. Rultan is the owner, sir. If you wish only a recipe, then perhaps the chef—"

"I was told Mr. Rultan was the most reliable source."

"He is very busy right now, sir."

Hawker tapped the twenty on the table without taking his eyes off the man.

The bill disappeared into the man's pantaloons as if by magic. "Yes, quite right, sir. I'm sure Mr. Rultan would be only too happy to help you."

Hawker followed the waiter's directions through the dark restaurant. A beaded curtain covered the entrance of the hall that led past the kitchen. The cook—a short, hugely fat man out of a Sidney Green-street movie—stood in the hall squinting through cigarette smoke, talking to a very pretty East Indian girl who couldn't have been older that eighteen.

They immediately fell silent at Hawker's approach.

Hawker put on his best I'm-harmless-and-happy-to-be-here smile. He asked politely, "Could one of you tell me where I can find a Mr. Rultan?"

The girl spoke. "You have an appointment with my father?"

"No, I'm just a customer. Love the food here, and I wanted to ask him if he . . . well, if he might be interested in selling the place."

The girl accepted the question as a compliment. She relaxed a little. "He should still be in his office. Just turn left at the end of the hall and knock on the door. But I really don't think he wants to sell."

She had been talking to the chef in what was probably Arabic. She spoke English with almost no accent.

"Can't hurt to try, can it?" Hawker said, still grinning.

"No . . . I suppose not. But I assure you that my father is quite happy with his present situation."

"I don't blame him a bit. But I think I'll introduce myself anyway."

Hawker felt the two watching him as he turned at the end of the hall.

At the end of the side hall he tapped on the door.

The response was immediate. "Phanti? Is that you, dear?"

Hawker guessed "Phanti" was the daughter.

"My name's Hawker, Mr. Rultan. James Hawker. And I'd like to talk to you," he said through the door.

The door cracked slightly. Hawker was peering into a pair of huge, bleary brown eyes above a portion of mustache. "What do you want?"

"I'd like to discuss a business proposition. It won't take long."

"I'm afraid I can't. I have another appointment in just a few minutes."

"I wanted to talk to you about buying your restaurant, Mr. Rultan."

"But I do not want to sell my restaurant, sir."

"You haven't heard my offer yet."

"I can only repeat that I do not wish to sell—and I certainly do not wish to speak to you. Good day."

Hawker had a hundred-dollar bill folded lengthways in his palm. He fished it through the door.

The man did not react as Hawker hoped he might. "Do you think I am a servant that can be bribed?" he said, angry. "I do not want your money! You Americans think you can buy everything!"

Hawker shrugged, turned as if to leave, then jammed his shoulder against the door. Inside there was a crash, and Hawker stepped in and locked the door behind him.

Rultan sat on the floor, his hands cupped to his face. His long nose dribbled blood. The door had hit him and knocked him down. "You son of a bitch!" he whined. "You have no right! No right at all!"

Hawker grabbed the man by the collar and forced him to his feet. "I just want to ask you a few questions, Rultan. Be nice to me and I'll be nice to you. Okay?"

He was a bird-boned man with jet-black hair, a pear-shaped face, dark doleful brown eyes. He wore a cream-colored suit jacket and slacks, and an open white shirt. "Questions? You want to ask me questions! You are a policeman?"

Hawker said nothing.

"But I have already told the police everything I know."

"But I'd like to hear it again, Rultan."

"Then I will call my lawyer. I do not have to subject myself to this harassment. I know my rights!" Rultan slid in behind his wooden desk, picked up the phone, and began to dial. "You have bloodied my nose, you son of a bitch! You have violated my rights! Let us see how tough you are when my lawyer arrives. We will have your badge!"

Hawker took his hands from his pockets and calmly pushed the phone's plunger down, cutting the Syrian off. He smiled easily. "I'm not a cop, Rultan. With me, you've got no rights. No right to make a phone call, no right to have a lawyer present, no right to do anything but tell me the truth."

"Not a policeman? But why—"

"Let's just say I'm real nosy. And I don't like assholes who bomb innocent people."

"I know nothing about those bombings!"

"The police decided to question you just because they had nothing better to do, huh?"

"They have questioned many people."

"I thought you didn't know anything, Rultan. How did you

know they've questioned many people? See how easy it is? I ask you a question, and you give me an answer."

"I will not submit to this bullying—"

Hawker's open hand made a hollow rim-shot sound as he backhanded the Syrian's head sideways. "I'll make you a deal, Rultan—don't talk back to me and I won't rearrange your face. Okay?"

The Syrian wiped the blood from the corner of his mouth. "Don't hit me again. Please. What do you want from me?"

"What do you think? I want information—like who's doing the bombing, for starters."

"I don't know."

Hawker leaned over the desk, his nose only inches from the Syrian's. "Then tell me who you *think* is doing it?"

"Someone from the Mideast," he said quickly. "Please do not think I am saying the obvious. There are groups in Saudi Arabia, in Africa, yes, in Israel, too, who are ruthless enough for such actions. That the terrorists say they are from the Mideast means nothing."

"But you think they are from there?"

"Yes."

"You're involved with some kind of Syrian government in exile, aren't you? Maybe it's your people who are doing the bombing: Is that why you don't want to talk?"

The Syrian's eyes shifted away from Hawker's, toward the beaded curtain that covered the window on the other side of the room. "My people? Don't be absurd."

"You're just a group of peace-loving, good ole Islamics, is that right?"

"Do not make sport of my people or my cause!" The man's face grew dark again, his fear overwhelmed by his anger. "In my place, you would do the same thing. Yes, it is true! If you only knew the truth, you, too, would plot the overthrow of the present Syrian government. It is for my people . . . for my daughter that we will never cease the struggle. In my country the Kurdish and Armenian peoples are being treated as second-class citizens by the Arabic-speaking majority. And do you know why? It is because we work harder! We fare much better in business! But Arabics will not tolerate such industry. They steal our property, they usurp our lands. How can I ever hope to return my daughter to the homeland under such conditions?"

Hawker thought of the smoky, Eastern beauty of the girl he had seen in the hall. He took a closer look at Rultan: small man in his late thirties, eyes bleary with discontent; a driven man separated from his homeland. Hawker felt a trickle of regret for the strong-arm methods he had used, but immediately shoved the regret out of his mind.

He had to be ruthless. Innocent people were being murdered, and he had to find out who was doing it. Sometimes a little brutality could save a lot of time.

"So if your people aren't doing it, Rultan, who is?"

Again the man's eyes shifted.

Hawker leaned closer, his hands clenched into fists. "You know a hell of a lot more than you told the cops, Rultan. You're an affluent businessman, a respected member of the Mideastern community here. And word travels fast in a small community. These bastards are killing innocent women and children. Doesn't that bother you?"

"Of course!"

"Then what in the hell are you afraid of? Why don't you talk! I'm not with any agency. I'm acting strictly alone. Tell me what you know, and I guarantee there's absolutely no chance you'll be called in for more questioning or made to testify."

The Syrian clasped his hands together with emotion. "Do you not understand? They would find out. *They* would know. It is not my own life for which I fear, it is the life of my daughter, Phanti, that I—"

"Who is it, damn it! The Iranians? The Iraqis—"

"I will not sentence my own daughter to be tortured!"

Hawker grabbed the man by the collar and pulled him out of the chair. "They're due to bomb again within the next three days. At least tell me where! Or would you rather be tortured by me?"

Rultan took a deep breath, his eyes focused beyond Hawker. For a long time, he said nothing. Finally, he answered, "I cannot tell you exactly when the bombings will take place. It is the truth. But there are some things that I have heard, heard not from the people planting the bombs, but from friends on the street. They may just be rumors—"

"What is it? What did you hear?"

"I have heard that it would be unwise for a person from my country to be found driving through the suburb of Wells Church on Friday—"

The gunshot came from the window behind Hawker. It was instantaneous with the sound of shattering glass. Rultan's head was catapulted backward in a blur of spray, as if he had been hit in the face with a tomato.

The impact of the slug knocked him out of his chair. Hawker tumbled over the desk after him, and came up on his knees, his own gun drawn.

The curtain of beads was still moving. A dank breeze blew through the broken window.

Hawker ran to the window and shoved the beads away. He poked his head out into the alleyway.

No one was there.

Rultan had said that he had another appointment. He had not been lying. Hawker wondered who the appointment was with.

The person he was supposed to meet was probably the murderer.

From the hall, someone was banging frantically on the door. A girl's voice called out, "Father? Are you all right, Father? Unlock this door, please!"

Hawker returned to the dead man's desk and rummaged around until he found the appointment calendar.

The writing was in Arabic.

As someone in the hall began to throw a heavy shoulder against the door, Hawker stepped through the window into the alley.

Halfway to the street he put his gun away, straightened his jacket, then stepped calmly into the flow of sidewalk traffic.

He was anxious to get to his rental car and have a look at Wells Church. Later, he could try to find someone he could trust who could read Arabic . . .

SEVEN

On Friday evening the three students waited until the dorm was almost empty.

In May, in Washington, D.C., the weekends are filled with fraternity parties and sorority parties at colleges around the city. Beer sales are brisk, and no one stays in.

They didn't have to wait long.

By 8 P.M. the halls were empty, and the three students took the elevator to the lobby, then slipped through the door into the cellar.

They pushed aside the carefully placed box that guarded the open window. It was a tampon crate—a joke enjoyed by the American students because the box guarded the window they used to sneak in women.

This time, Mosul Aski, the leader, went first. Zanjen went last. And Karaj, who was very fat, had plenty of help from both ends when he got stuck.

They walked across the commons area to Nebraska Avenue. There they hailed a cab. They gave the driver an address.

When they were sure they were not being followed, they canceled the first address and told the driver where they really wanted to go.

The driver dropped them at the corner of New Hampshire Avenue and Sixteenth Avenue—not far from the White House. The three students sat on a bench, watching the traffic go by.

Finally, a large brown truck stopped on the street in front of them. On the side of the truck was painted DONGEL'S LAUNDRY/WE DELIVER.

Last week they had been picked up by a pizza delivery truck. The week before that it was a U.S. Postal Service truck. All of the trucks had been stolen and repainted by believers in their cause.

Mosul looked both ways, then threw open the back doors of the laundry truck and waved his friends inside.

They rode along in silence for just under fifteen minutes.

Then the truck stopped, and Mosul knew they were at the gate of Ambassador Isfahan Shiraz's estate. Isfahan maintained higher security at his estate than did some embassies. His guards would be calling inside for clearance. It would, of course, be given. The engine revved and the truck jolted into the compound.

The truck pulled around to the back of the three-story brick house, and the three students got out.

Several of their friends were waiting for them, men who worked inside the estate and rarely ventured out.

They greeted one another warmly while they unloaded the components for the bombs, speaking in Persian, the language of their homeland.

Upstairs, the party atmosphere ended abruptly when Isfahan—Ambassador Isfahan Shiraz—entered the room. He was a thin stately man with dark, deep, cavernous eyes. He wore the native religious robes of his country, but he sat on the divan with his legs crossed like an American.

"My dear Mosul," he began, speaking in Persian, "let me first congratulate you, Zanjen, and Karaj on the great success of your last mission."

The other men in the room clicked their tongues loudly, which was their way of applauding.

He continued, "You have killed many of the infidels, and Allah will no doubt smile kindly upon you for your brave deeds. I think I may also say that your names are not unfamiliar to the leaders in our homeland. Here, I can only embrace you as brothers. But when you return home, you will be properly rewarded!"

Over the clicking of tongues, Mosul said, "We have had our reward, oh, Father. Every week, the American televisions cry out the names of the pigs punished by our swords. That is all the reward we seek. And let us pray that we may continue to fight so that, someday, we may spit upon the graves of every last imperialist!"

The ambassador nodded his approval. This Mosul was like few other youths of his generation. So brave, so filled with the fire of battle, and such a noble speaker. People were already predicting his greatness. Isfahan, who took great pride in his own fervor, could not disagree. Truly, Mosul Aski would one day take his seat as the spiritual and political ruler of the homeland. But for now he was still a subordinate, and Isfahan's ego could not let the boy forget that.

As Isfahan sat on the couch, he decided that an unexpected change of orders might demonstrate to the entire room that he was still in charge.

"Yes, Mosul," he began easily, "we are all very proud of your great deeds. With each successful mission, the world is once again reminded of our holy cause."

"And tonight we will remind the world again!" Mosul put in, smiling.

"Yes, that is so. But I have made a decision. You have become very valuable to our work. Your worth to me as a trusted aide is beyond measure. Who else knows more about the bombing procedures than you?"

"I have tried my best," Mosul said warily, wondering what the older man was getting at.

"Without question, dear Mosul. But it is for that very reason that, tonight, I am replacing your team with another team. A new group of warriors—"

"But why, oh, Father? Have we failed in some way?"

"Have I said so? Of course you have not failed. But it is my wish that your other brothers have an opportunity to take their revenge on the American pigs. They, too, must have a chance to familiarize themselves with the procedures. Most of them rarely get the chance to even leave the confines of my estate. Let us think of them!"

Mosul's protestations were quickly smothered by the noise of the other men pleading with Isfahan for a chance to lead that night's bombing mission.

Outwardly, Mosul appeared to be pleased by Isfahan's choice. He cheered for the five men picked to go in place of his team. He offered advice and helped lead them through the procedure. He told them how to choose a home—if they did not already have one in mind. He told them the best place to plant the bombs, how to set the timers, and the best method of escaping in their vehicle, which, tonight, would be the laundry truck. He told them how they must be sure to carry nothing that could possibly be used to identify them, and how it was important to fight to the death in the event they were caught.

He let no one in the embassy see how disappointed he was, but all the way back to the dormitory he sulked. Zanjen and Karaj pretended not to notice, but they, too, felt betrayed by Isfahan. They separated wordlessly and went to their rooms.

Later, much later, Mosul got up silently from his bed, dressed, and took a loaded .38 Smith & Wesson from beneath the bureau where he kept it taped. He had purchased the weapon from a Negro on the street, and he was quite sure it was stolen.

The moon was half full, quite bright, and there was plenty of light on the night streets of Washington.

Walking with his hands stuffed in his jacket pockets, he came upon three potential victims, all men, all alone.

But each time, just before he drew the gun, Mosul lost his nerve. They were men—what if he only wounded them? If he did not kill them with the first shot, they might beat him or, worse, they might be carrying guns themselves.

Mosul decided it was too dangerous to attack grown men—even with a revolver.

Finally, he passed a young woman on a dark street. She was wearing a dress and a bright corsage beneath her sweater.

Perhaps she was a college girl walking home after a fight with her date.

Mosul stopped. "Excuse me," he said, exaggerating his difficulty with English, "could you please be telling me which direction it is in to go to the Lincoln Memorial?"

The girl stopped. "What?"

Mosul repeated what he had said.

The girl smiled. "Oh, you're from another country, aren't you? I can tell by your accent." She took several steps toward him. "Yes, the Lincoln Memorial is about ten blocks from here. You turn left at the—"

She stopped talking when she saw the gun. Her voice became very small. "What . . . what are you doing? What do you want from me?"

Mosul did not answer.

He smiled, and the girl relaxed a little. Perhaps the young man was just joking.

He wasn't. Mosul aimed the gun and shot her once in the face. The girl moaned in agony when she hit the cement.

Then he stood over her, held the gun to her head, and pulled the trigger twice.

The girl's legs kicked violently, then she lay still.

Mosul Aski wiped the barrel of the gun on her dress, put the gun in his pocket, then walked calmly back to the dormitory.

He had been angry about being removed from the bombing team. Now he felt much better . . .

EIGHT

James Hawker was tired. The dead Syrian, Rultan, had not been very specific.

He had said the suburb of Wells Church would be a bad place for someone from the Mideast to be found on Friday.

Rultan had not been allowed to finish his sentence. He had not told Hawker *when* on Friday.

Death had cut him short.

Hawker could only assume that the terrorists would strike during darkness.

But there is a lot of darkness on both sides of a day.

After leaving the Eastern Chalice Restaurant, Hawker had stopped at his apartment, showered, changed clothes, and picked up a few select pieces of weaponry. Then he drove to Wells Church. Wells Church was just west of D.C., a suburb of Colonial houses, ivy walls, and historical markers.

Hawker stopped at the telephone company. He told the girl at the counter he had just moved into town. She gave him a telephone book, a local business directory, and a street map.

Using the map, Hawker drove around the streets of the suburb, familiarizing himself with the area.

Then he ate dinner (lamb chops, new potatoes, salad, and iced tea) at a Colonial-style restaurant where George Washington never slept.

Finally, just before sunset, Hawker leafed through the business directory and found two places where they sold telescopes. The first place didn't have one that looked quite impressive enough.

Hawker found just what he wanted at the second place, a camera/optics shop run by a Hasidic Jew named Olaf.

It would have taken a nice little bite out of the money in the envelope, so Hawker used a credit card. It was necessary. To be a good disguise the telescope had to be convincing. The one he bought was a six-inch reflector with a Newtonian optical system, a fork mount, and a clock drive. The telescope stood about four feet high, with a gray tripod and a red barrel.

Then he telephoned the only number Lester Rehfuss had given him. A woman answered.

"High Tech Diversified. Can I help you?"

Despite the greeting, Hawker knew he was not talking to an electronics firm.

He was talking to a Stage One operator at the CIA's traffic headquarters.

Hawker replied as he had been instructed. "Yes, this is Mr. James. I think you were expecting a call from me?"

"Can you hold on for a minute, Mr. James?"

The phone clicked, and Hawker knew the operator would first check with the computer to make sure he was on the phone list. Then she would test the connection for any hint of electrical resistance, making sure there was no phone tap on his line.

Finally, she returned. "Yes, Mr. James, we were expecting a call from you. Is your business going satisfactorily?"

"It's going pretty well. But I need to get a message to Mr. Lester. It's important. I want you to tell him that I had nothing to do with eliminating that problem at the restaurant this afternoon. I don't want to claim credit for something I didn't do."

"Very commendable, Mr. James. Is there anything else?"

"Yeah. Tell him I'm not sure who did it."

"I'll pass your message along, Mr. James."

"Oh, and one more thing. Tell him those foreign visitors we're expecting are supposed to be in Wells Church sometime after midnight tonight, or Friday night. I'm not sure when. I'd like to meet them personally, but it's my night off and I'll be out with my new telescope. You know what an astronomy buff I am."

"Your new telescope?"

"That's exactly right. It's a real beauty and I can't wait to try it. I'll be in Wells Church doing some stargazing, so I think Mr. Lester ought to get his best people to meet the foreign visitors. I'd do it myself, but I hate to be bothered when I'm tracking."

"Tracking?"

"Asteroids. There's a minor shower expected near Arcturus. You might tell Mr. Lester about my new telescope. He'll like it—it's red."

"Red? How nice. I will pass your message along the moment he comes in, Mr. James. Happy stargazing."

When Hawker hung up the phone, he carried the telescope back to his rental car.

Chances were that the terrorists wouldn't hit until the next night, Friday night. But Hawker knew there was an outside possibility they might strike early Friday morning, between midnight and dawn.

Enough innocent people around D.C. had been murdered by these lunatics. That's exactly why Hawker had told the CIA traffic operator that Lester Rehfuss should have his men out in force. Wells Church wasn't a big suburb, but it was big enough, and Hawker wasn't about to take the chance of missing the bombers.

One man alone couldn't watch all the streets in the area.

Hawker tried to put himself in the place of the terrorists. Before they selected a house and planted their bombs, they would certainly drive around the area first to make sure the place wasn't crawling with cops.

It didn't take him long to find a centralized area that would be a likely place to pick up the scent of the bombers. It was in the center of town, a park square with trees, a ball diamond, and a bandstand.

It would be unlikely they would make a reconnaissance drive through Wells Church without circling the park.

Hawker stopped at a take-out and bought a half-dozen roast beef and ham sandwiches, two Thermoses of coffee, another Thermos of iced tea, and some toilet tissue.

At dusk he parked on the east side of the park. He figured the terrorists would probably be coming from D.C., so the east side of the park would be the most likely place to see them.

How he would recognize them as terrorists, Hawker didn't know. It seemed unlikely they would wear black hats or Simon Legree mustaches.

But he had to try.

The vigilante set up his telescope in an open area in plain sight. He placed the sandwiches and the coffee beneath the bench, and then he sat and watched darkness take the suburb.

When Venus materialized above the orange afterglow, Hawker focused the telescope on it, then on the waxing moon.

During the next twelve hours he was approached twice by city cops, nine times by homosexuals, and once by a woman who was not a prostitute.

He found it troubling that homosexuals had traveled so much farther from the closet than liberated women.

No matter who he was approached by, Hawker did the same routine each time: he clamped his eye to the eyepiece of the telescope and began to mutter to himself like Fred Mac-Murray just before he invented Flubber.

The homosexuals were intrigued, the woman was bored, and the cops were indifferent.

Eggheads with telescopes didn't cause many problems.

That's just what Hawker wanted them to think.

He left the telescope three times to follow different vehicles that he thought might contain terrorists: two trucks and a van.

Each time, he was wrong.

He returned to his apartment at dawn, dead tired, his head still spinning from all the coffee he had drunk, hoping like hell the bombers hadn't slipped past him . . .

NINE

The next night Hawker was back at the park with his telescope. On the street he noticed a marked increase in the number of unmarked government cars and square-jawed men in sunglasses.

Rehfuss had gotten Hawker's message.

The CIA was out in force—and the vigilante hoped like hell he was the only one to notice.

More than once, CIA types gave Hawker steely looks as they passed him by. But they never stopped. They had their orders: leave the guy with the red telescope alone.

Hawker was relieved.

If there was one organization in the world he didn't want after him, it was the CIA.

The hours ticked by. He ate more sandwiches, drank more coffee. The telescope was superb. Between watching cars, he got breathtaking views of the moons of Jupiter and the Great Nebulae of Orion.

The beauty of the galaxy dwarfed the madness of tiny

Earth, and relegated terrorist baby-killers to the level of primal slime.

Hawker looked forward to getting his hands on the bastards.

At about 3 A.M. he noticed the fourth suspicious vehicle of the evening. It was a square-backed truck, a laundry truck marked DONGEL'S LAUNDRY/WE DELIVER.

Hawker tried to remember a laundry truck that didn't read "We *pick up* and deliver."

How could a laundry truck deliver if it didn't pick up?

It was a small thing. But, at 3 A.M., the small things stood out. Knowing perfectly well that he was getting a little punch-drunk from lack of sleep and too much coffee, Hawker decided to follow the laundry truck.

What could it hurt?

There were CIA men everywhere.

Besides, he hadn't followed a suspicious vehicle for more than two hours and he was getting bored standing in the park.

Hawker packed the telescope neatly away. He got into his rental Ford and went out into the empty streets, several blocks behind the laundry truck.

He did not turn on his headlights.

As he drove he noticed with a chill that as the truck moved into a residential area, it, too, switched out its lights. The truck was painted brown, so all Hawker could see was the occasional moon-flash of chrome.

He pressed the accelerator down.

The terrorists had to be in the laundry truck.

James Hawker was determined to get to them before the CIA did . . .

TEN

The vigilante tried to stay well behind them, afraid the terrorists might sense a trap and flee before he had a chance to get them in his sights.

The obvious danger was that he would stay too far back and lose them.

That's exactly what happened.

Half a mile ahead, he saw the laundry truck's brake lights flare briefly before turning left down a residential street. The street was a cavern of big trees. By the time Hawker got there, the truck had disappeared in the darkness.

Hawker gunned the Ford. At the first cross street, he skidded to a stop. He looked both ways. No laundry truck. He spun the wheels, sprinting to the next stop sign. Still no truck.

They had disappeared.

Hawker drove three more blocks, turned left, and switched on his lights. He pulled out the map he had gotten at the telephone company. The only dead-end streets were two blocks over, by the golf course.

The terrorists could have turned anywhere, gone anywhere.

Damn it!

The only hope he had was that the men in the laundry truck would double back on their reconnaissance route, and he could pick them up at the city park again.

If that failed he would have to track down one of the CIA people and tell them to put out an all-points on the laundry truck. More innocent people weren't going to be bombed just because of his stupidity!

Hawker shoved the car in gear and headed away. He forced himself to drive at a reasonable speed. He retraced his route around the block, cut down a strange street that should have brought him out on Jefferson, the main road.

Halfway down the block sat the laundry truck. It was parked at the curb, lights out.

Hawker caught himself just before he jammed on the brakes.

He drove right on past the truck at an even speed. He touched his turn signal at the stop sign and headed out toward the main road.

It was 3:34 A.M.

He drove four blocks, shut out his lights, turned around in a driveway, and backtracked another two blocks before he pulled over and got out of the car.

Hawker switched out the dome light before he opened the back door. He pulled up the seat and removed his black wool sweater, his Navy watch cap, his canvas satchel, which he wore around his chest like a bandolier, and his thin black

66

leather gloves. He pulled on the sweater, then touched his calf to make sure the Randall Model 18 Attack/Survival knife was still in place, strapped to his leg.

It was.

Then he buckled on the Colt .44 magnum in its shoulder holster, and hefted the Colt Commando automatic rifle. The Colt was a chopped-down version of the M16. It still fired the 5.56-mm rounds, but the stock slid in so that it was only twenty-eight inches long. It carried a twenty-round detachable box-type clip, and it had an effective killing range of two hundred meters. He had plenty of fresh clips taped back-to-back, for easy loading.

Hawker had used the Colt Commando before, and he trusted it.

The only customizing he had done was to add a Star-Tron Mark 303A night-vision scope. The Star-Tron absorbed all peripheral light—light from the stars, the moon, the streetlights—and regenerated it so that it made objects seen through the scope appear as bright as if they were being seen at high noon on a cloudy day.

Hawker switched on the Star-Tron and scanned the area ahead of him.

Through the red glow of the scope, he saw nothing but a stray cat stalking something near a garbage can. He didn't expect to see the terrorists—the laundry truck was still two blocks away, around the corner.

Hawker closed the door of the Ford gently and jogged across the street into the shadows of the sidewalk. The houses here were big and substantial: two-story brick or clapboard executive strongholds with vast lawns mowed like golf greens. Halfway down the block, Hawker cut through one of the yards to the back. He planned to approach the laundry truck from the rear of the nearest house.

Fences divided the yards, and Hawker climbed the front section of fence and slid down the other side. In the enclosed yard was a pool, a bonsai-style rock garden, and a barbecue grill. He climbed over the back section of fence to the yard of the next house. It had a pool, a tennis court, and a hot tub.

Hawker reflected that it was no wonder there were so many poor people in America—the bureaucrats got paid too much.

He shouldn't have wasted the time in reflection.

The yard had something else besides a pool and a hot tub.

Hawker heard the low growl before he saw the dog coming at him—dogs coming. Two German shepherds, not one. Hawker vaulted over the next fence as their teeth clicked at his ankle.

The vigilante sat on the ground breathing heavily. From the other side of the fence the dogs yammered at him. He expected lights to start blinking on all over the neighborhood.

They didn't, though. It was 3:46 A.M. by the pale glow of his Seiko. Wells Church was deafened by sleep.

Hawker stood. Before him was a rambling ranch-style house on a large chunk of lawn. Trees grew on both sides of the house, and there was no fence. If he had to pick a house in this neighborhood to bomb, it would be this one. Easy access and plenty of cover.

Through the trees the vigilante could see the outline of the laundry truck.

Apparently the terrorists felt the same way about the house. They had chosen it as their target for the night.

Hawker lifted the Colt Commando and had a look through the Star-Tron. In the backyard was a swing set, a jungle gym, and a cement basketball court.

Judging from the varieties of playground equipment, Hawker guessed that at least two kids were asleep inside the house, possibly more.

His hands tightened on the automatic rifle as he scanned the rest of the area.

He stopped abruptly. He could see a man creeping along the yard near the bushes. The man's face seemed to be horribly disfigured, but then Hawker realized he was wearing a stocking tied over his head.

He dragged some kind of knapsack along beside him.

It would be a bomb, of course. A satchel bomb? Perhaps a variation of a satchel bomb.

Hawker brought the glowing red cross hairs of the Star-Tron to bear on the man's temple. He held the sight there for a moment, then lowered the rifle.

If he shot now he would spook the rest of the terrorists. Hawker touched the safety tang to make sure it was switched to full automatic, then he slid along the shadows of a high copse. When he was about fifteen yards from the man, he stopped again. The terrorist had removed the bomb from the knapsack, and now was affixing it beneath one of the windows, a bedroom window, probably.

Hawker placed the Colt Commando on the ground. He pulled up his pant cuff, unsnapped the handmade scabbard, and drew the Randall knife. The weight of the stainless-steel hilt felt good in his gloved hand. He moved slowly, quietly across the grass toward the man in the stocking mask. When Hawker was close enough to smell the sour-sweat odor of the man's body, he threw his arm around the terrorist's throat and touched the point of the Randall to his ear.

The man struggled briefly.

"*Freeze*, asshole. Not a sound," Hawker whispered into his ear. "Say one word, and I'll use this knife to scramble what few brains you have."

The man stopped struggling and went stiff with fear. "Please, don't hurt me," he said, his bad English made harder to understand by the stocking over his head. "There is no need to hurt me. I have done nothing."

"Let me guess, greaseball—you're a desert Santa Claus, way early for Christmas." Hawker shook him roughly. "Don't lie to me, you scum. What time is that bomb set to go off?"

"Bomb? I know of no bomb—"

Hawker clamped his hand over the man's mouth and put just enough pressure on the knife so it slid about a quarter inch into the man's ear canal. Blood began to run in a shiny black river down the side of the terrorist's neck. The man's scream was muffled.

Hawker waited a few seconds, then removed his hand. "Let's call that a friendly warning, penis nose. With me, you get only one friendly warning. Then I get unfriendly. Real unfriendly."

"Oh, god, you poked that knife clear into my head. Please don't hurt me anymore, please don't hurt me." The man was crying, sobbing like a baby.

Hawker shook him again. "You're a real tough guy, aren't you? You've got no problem murdering kids, but when it comes to someone hurting you, you blubber like somebody's spoiled brat." The vigilante slapped him hard on the face. "When's the bomb supposed to go off, damn it? Tell me!"

"The bomb . . . the bomb is supposed to explode in—"

The terrorist's words were blotted out by a succession of noises. From the street came the screech of tires, the sudden blast of a siren, and the flare of flashing blue lights. Through the side yard Hawker could see two cops jump out of their squad car, service revolvers pressed between both hands. The weapons were apparently pointed at terrorists Hawker could not see. "Police, *FREEZE!*" one of them yelled.

Then there was the muffled chain-rattle thud of automatic weapons firing through sound arresters. Both cops doubled belly-first toward the ground, their faces gray with shock, their hands holding in the viscera that threatened to escape from the black line of bullet holes in their stomachs . . .

ELEVEN

Watching the brutal murder of the police was a mistake, but Hawker couldn't seem to pull his eyes away from the carnage.

The terrorists kept the guns turned on the fallen cops far longer than they needed to.

The unseen gunmen made the two fresh corpses jump on the asphalt as if they were electrified.

Why in the hell had the cops stopped? Had someone called in a suspicious-activity report? Were they working on a tip from the feds?

No way of knowing.

And Hawker didn't get much time to think about it.

Sensing the vigilante's lapse in concentration, the man he held kicked backward savagely, his heel clipping Hawker's groin. Hawker clamped his knees together and twisted away involuntarily. The terrorist shook free, then hit Hawker a slapping, panicky blow to the face. He could have drawn the little .38 Police Special he carried and finished the vigilante, but he ran instead, stumbling awkwardly into a sprint.

Groaning, Hawker got to his feet and gave chase. The terrorist was neither a fighter nor a runner. Hawker caught him before he reached the corner of the house, tackling him from behind. The terrorist slapped at his belt, pulled out his weapon, and Hawker turned his face away just as the little revolver exploded.

The powder discharge burned his face . . . the noise made his ears ring . . . but the slug missed him.

Hawker didn't give him a chance to shoot again. He thrust the seven-and-a-half-inch blade of the Randall knife into the soft area under the man's chin, shoved until the point of the knife hit the back of his skull, then twisted.

The terrorist's muscles contracted violently, twitching like a bug on the end of a needle.

Hawker withdrew the knife, wiped it on the grass. He half-jogged and half-limped back to the bomb, which hung beneath a back window of the house, his stomach still rolling from the kick to the groin.

The bomb was about the size of a desktop radio, encased in metal and painted some dark color. Hawker pulled a tiny flashlight from his knapsack and studied the bomb carefully without touching it.

Then, from within the house, he heard a woman scream, then the wild, sleepy wail of a child. A man yelled something unintelligible, and there was a quick burst of automatic rifle fire.

Hawker switched off the light and jammed it back into the bag.

Shit!

There was no time to study the bomb now. He could see

the situation taking shape: the cops had interrupted the terrorists, and had died for their trouble. But the dead policemen had undoubtedly called in their location, and probably had reported the license number of the delivery truck as well. When they failed to report in, more cops would be dispatched.

The terrorists would know this, and they would also know there was no escape for them.

So now they had broken into the house and taken hostages. They would hope to bargain their way out, or at least have the chance to get plenty of free air time on the national news to plead whatever Mideastern cause with which they were associated.

Hawker knew what would happen when their plea for amnesty was refused.

They would begin killing people inside—if they hadn't already killed them all.

The bomb would have to wait—not that he could do anything to defuse it. Back at the police academy he had had one short course on bomb disposal, but that had been woefully incomplete. He could deal with the simple, homemade bombs. But this thing looked far too complex for an amateur to go rummaging about in it.

A woman screamed again from the other side of the house.

Hawker ran toward the far window where a light was now on. He knew he had to get to the terrorists, and get to them before they began thinking clearly. If he could hit them before they had a chance to get organized, he might be able to turn their attention to him and make them forget about the hostages.

Later, he could worry about how to escape the police.

Right now, though, he was the only chance that the Americans inside had.

Hawker poked his nose up over the windowsill. He had a thin field of vision through the slit beneath the shade. He saw a boy of about nine and a girl of about seven cringing in the corner as a woman in a sheer nightgown came tripping into the room. She was followed by a man with dark olive skin and the standard black mustache of every male from the Middle East. Cradled in his arms he carried an Uzi submachine gun. But it was the expression on his face that worried Hawker the most. His expression was a combination of terror and panic. He was frightened, but he also had the cold light of the fanatic in his eyes. Between the fear and the fervor, this guy would be as dangerous as a human being could be.

And Hawker had no doubt that the other terrorists were exactly the same way.

The young man shoved the woman again, and she fell out of Hawker's sight—probably on a bed. When she stood up, she tried to hold the nightgown together where the bodice had ripped. She was a dark-haired woman in her middle thirties, very pretty, with finely textured cheeks and chin, and large brown eyes. As she stood, the man grabbed her by the shoulders and shoved her again.

This time, the nightgown ripped away, leaving her naked and sobbing. She held her arms against her chest, but they could not cover entirely the heavy swell of her breasts. They were like soft, pale melons, and they made her shoulders and waist seem smaller, almost girlish.

"Leave my mommy alone!" yelled the little boy. He charged

the terrorist, his small fists hammering at the man's thighs. The terrorist yelled something, then bunched his fist and hit the little boy very hard in the face. The boy flew backward and landed on the floor, sprawled like a rag doll.

"Ryan!" screamed the black-haired woman, lurching toward him.

The terrorist brushed along the window, trying to cross the room ahead of her and cut her off.

Hawker had had enough. When the terrorist's backside touched the window where the vigilante's eye was pressed, Hawker acted without thinking. He slammed his gloved fist through the glass, grabbed the terrorist's baggy trousers, and hauled him backward through the jagged window.

The terrorist landed on the ground with a *whoof* as the automatic rifle flew out of his hands. The terrorist looked at Hawker in shock and surprise. The glass had cut a gouge out of his cheek so that a flap of skin hung down, exposing the back section of his gums and molars. The stocking over his face was already sodden with blood, and the blood poured down over his neck and dark shirt. The terrorist gave an animal growl that made blood bubble from the hole in his face. He dove toward the Uzi, but Hawker stopped him with a brutal kick to the face.

The impact smashed the terrorist's nose. The flesh turned a florid white, then it, too, began to pour blood.

"You son of a bitch!" the terrorist called. His facial injuries gave his voice a weird vibration. He sounded like a Munchkin with a bass voice. "You will be killed for this! We shall punish—"

There was now a cold fury in Hawker. He had no interest

in hearing the olive-skinned man finish his litany. Using the steel butt of the Colt Commando like a stave, he knocked the man's jaw crooked, then clubbed down hard on the back of his head, feeling the cranium splinter into the soft brain-jelly within.

The terrorist slumped backward and did not move again.

Hawker hurried back to the window. He used the Commando to knock away the rest of the glass, then pulled himself up into the room.

The naked, black-haired woman was stooped over her young son. The little girl watched in terror as Hawker walked toward them. He smiled and held his hand out, as one might hold a hand out to a shy puppy. "It's okay, little girl," he said softly. "I'm a friend. I'm not going to hurt you."

The woman looked at him with outrage, then looked quickly back at her son. "What in the hell is going on here!" she shouted, her eyes wild. "Why won't you people let us get some sleep? Just leave my family alone, for god's sake!"

The woman was incoherent with shock, but Hawker didn't have time to cajole her out of it. He needed information, and he needed it immediately if any of them were to survive.

"Is your husband dead?" he asked.

"Dead?" the woman answered with an eerie, distant tone. "What an absurd question! They pretended to shoot him, but they didn't, of course. My husband went along with it. What else could he do? These people are insane. We must do what they want us to do!"

The little girl began to sob, her face buried in her mother's long hair.

Hawker read between the lines.

The husband was dead. The woman couldn't accept it. The child, though, knew the truth.

"How many more of them are there?"

"How many more of those men?" the woman asked.

"Yes, of course."

"Three . . . maybe four. They really are awful men. Why would a grown man hit a little boy?"

Something in the woman's face touched Hawker deeply. Her expression was not unlike that of a child asking why there was evil in the world. James Hawker took her arm gently. "May I take a look at your little boy?" he asked.

"Are you a doctor?"

"No. I'm a friend."

"You won't hurt him?"

"No, of course not."

"Then you may look at him."

He took the little boy from the woman's arms. The boy was small and warm in the big man's arms. Hawker touched his ear to the tiny chest. It was a long moment before he picked up the faint heartbeat. Then the vigilante slid open the child's right eyelid. Hawker was relieved to see the pupil dilate properly in the light of the bedroom.

Hawker handed the boy back to the woman. He stripped a blanket off the bed and draped it around her nakedness. He said, "I think your little boy is going to be okay. But he still needs to be looked at by a physician. Understand? You three are leaving through the window—"

"But my husband—"

"I'll send him later. But if you want your children to live, you will listen to me. I have to hurry, so please listen carefully. Okay?"

The woman nodded.

"Good. I'll help you through the window. When you're through, run just as fast as you can to a neighbor's house. Do you have a good friend who is a neighbor?"

The woman nodded, some life returning to her face. "Helen Beardsley, two houses down."

"Good. Take the kids there. Now comes the important part—listen carefully. I want you to have your friend call every neighbor in the area and tell them to evacuate the area immediately. Get them the hell away from this block."

"But why—"

"Because your house is rigged with bombs, and I have no way to stop them. Remember, if you want your kids to live, do just what I tell you. All right?"

The woman's eyes were damp with anger, fear, and shock, but she nodded.

"And one more thing," Hawker added. "I want you to forget that you ever saw me. Please. That's all I ask in return for saving your lives."

"You're not a policeman?" the woman asked slowly.

"No."

"You're not . . . not one of them?"

The vigilante smiled. "Hardly. Let's just say I'm a friend you never met until now. Please, you really do need to hurry. The other guys will be coming soon. They'll be wanting some help. More policemen will be coming soon, and those men are going to have to make a fight of it."

Hawker helped her out the window, then handed the little girl and the unconscious boy out to her. He heard the woman's quick intake of breath when she saw the brutally beaten corpse of the terrorist.

"Hurry," Hawker whispered, "don't stop for anything. Make that neighbor of yours drive you the hell away from here. Understand?"

"But what about you?" the woman asked blankly.

Hawker realized that in not asking about her husband again she had already accepted his death.

"I'll be fine," said the vigilante. "You don't have to worry about me. But those bastards who planted the bombs sure do . . ."

TWELVE

When the black-haired woman and her children were safely across the lawn, James Hawker cracked open the bedroom door and looked out into the hall. It was empty, but from the front of the house he could hear the clack and chatter of a language that sounded like Arabic, though he couldn't be sure.

Quickly, he tried to formulate some plan of action. If the woman was right there were as many as four terrorists left—and it wouldn't be wise to confront that many armed men at once. On the other hand the cops would be arriving soon, and there wasn't much doubt about what they would do. They would surround the place, bring in choppers, SWAT teams, a bomb squad—everything but the Marines.

Once the cops were in position there would be no escape for Hawker. And Maxwell Percival had made it all too clear that, if he was caught, he would face the consequences without any help from the CIA.

The vigilante ex-cop toyed with the idea of leaving the terrorists to their fate. The hostages had already been freed. The cops didn't know that, but in time they would figure it out and storm the place. Then the terrorists would be arrested and . . . and what?

Spend the next year on the front pages of the nation's papers pleading their "cause" while they waited to be brought to trial—that's what. Hawker's imagination raced ahead. As prisoners in an American penitentiary system, they would be looked upon as martyrs by their countrymen. More than likely, American hostages would then be taken in hopes of making a deal for an exchange.

Hawker's jaw grew tight.

When all his options were considered, facing the four terrorists alone seemed the least of all the evils.

He couldn't let these murderers become the news darlings of Dan Rather and his ilk.

And there was only one way to prevent that from happening.

Hawker touched the safety tang on the Colt Commando, once again checking to make sure it was on full automatic. Then he slid quietly into the hall.

The terrorists seemed to be arguing among themselves—Hawker had no idea about what. Their voices came from the front room, the living room, and Hawker knew they must be waiting en masse to confront the police. But then he heard something else . . . the punch-and-chime sound of someone at a push-button phone.

Hawker stopped midway down the hall, listening.

Without warning, the loud foreign voices stopped abruptly.

The vigilante couldn't figure it out at first, but then he realized that they, too, wanted to listen to the conversation on the telephone.

It was a brief conversation. There was a flutter of Arabic followed by silence, followed by another staccato rush of words, then more silence.

The phone clicked down.

Hawker was surprised that the caller now spoke in English.

"Isfahan is very angry," the man said, his voice thick with emotion. "He is very angry at all of us. I told him we tried our best, and that it wasn't our fault—"

"What does he want us to do, damn it! Quit your blubbering and tell us!"

"He said . . . he said that we must not be taken alive."

"That is all our leader said to you?"

"No . . . no. He said that we must kill our hostages now. He said that we then must fight the police and kill as many of them as possible. We must defend this house until . . ."

"Until what!"

"Until the bombs explode. Isfahan said that by that time we will have drawn much attention. Reporters will have joined the police, and many spectators too. The bombs are strong enough . . . Many might be killed instead of just a few."

"And what about the statement? What kind of statement does Isfahan wish us to make?"

The first voice was silent for a moment. Then the man said in a near whisper, "Isfahan forbids us to make any statement."

"What?"

"It is true. He says . . . he says he does not trust us. He fears we may fail again. Isfahan is afraid that, in speaking, we may divulge the name of our homeland."

"Does he think we are children!" exclaimed a third voice in outrage. "He wishes us to die for our homeland, yet make no declaration of our faith? It is not fair!"

"But Isfahan is a holy man, our leader—"

"But it is not Isfahan who now faces death!"

"I agree. I feel Isfahan is wrong. For myself, I do not wish to die. Our orders were to blow up a house, not to fight men with guns. It is not that I am afraid of dying, but I do not wish to die without a declaration of faith. If we let ourselves be taken prisoner, we would be treated well—it is the way of the Americans to treat their enemies as they would their own. We would have a great opportunity to speak of our cause—"

"You cannot make that decision!" said another. "Isfahan has given us our orders. Even if he hadn't, two of us are not present. Yezd is still outside arranging the bombs, and Baijan is with the woman and her piglets."

There was a short silence. Hawker knew what they were thinking. Where had their friends gone? What was delaying them?

It was time to act.

So far, Hawker had counted only three voices. Perhaps the woman was wrong. Perhaps there had been only five in all: two that Hawker had killed, and the three remaining.

He moved silently down the hall. Off to his left was a room. An ornate table lamp glowed beside a massive bed. Beside the bed, a man in pajamas lay on the floor. It was the black-haired woman's husband. His pajama top was black with blood. Hawker looked at him for a moment, and was surprised when the man's arm moved. Then he saw the imperceptible heave of his chest.

The man was still alive. But he wouldn't last if he didn't get medical attention immediately.

Hawker knew he had to hurry—now time was doubly important.

At the hall opening he stopped and poked his head around the corner. The three terrorists all stood at the front window. They wore dark, baggy pants, and they had removed the stockings from their faces. Each held a stumpy Uzi submachine gun. All three were peering anxiously out the window.

"Perhaps Yezd is having trouble with the bombs," one of them said.

"Yes. No doubt. But what about Baijan? We have not heard a word from him since he took the American woman to the back room."

One of the terrorists chuckled nervously. "Perhaps he is showing her what it is like to be bedded by a real man. I have heard that these American women are left restless and unsatisfied by their fat white he cows."

"Call him! Whatever he is doing, call him. We must all talk. We have a decision to make, and we will soon be hearing the sirens."

They all turned toward the hallway in unison—and stopped.

James Hawker stood before them.

The vigilante's appearance frightened them—as it would have frightened anyone. The sharp lines of his face stood out from the black watch cap and black sweater like chiseled marble. In his right hand he held the solid weight of the Colt .44 Magnum. In his left hand the Colt Commando automatic rifle was leveled at their bellies.

Hawker took three slow steps toward them, saying easily, "You can forget about talking to your two friends. They're indisposed right now."

"You . . . you have arrested them?" the man in the middle asked shakily.

"No. I didn't arrest them." Hawker paused before adding, "I killed them. And unless you want me to kill you, you'd better do exactly as I say."

"We wish to surrender anyway!" the man said brightly, dropping his Uzi on the rug. He jerked his head quickly at the others, and they did the same. "We are your prisoners. We ask only that we be tried fairly, in a court—"

"The only court you goat-eaters have is me!" Hawker snapped. He pointed the Colt Magnum at the face of the man doing the talking. "How many bombs are there?"

"Two . . . there are two, both outside."

"And what time are they set to go off?"

"At 4:30 A.M."

Hawker glanced at his watch. It was 3:58 A.M. With the revolver, he motioned toward the telephone on the desk by the window. "I want you to dial 911, the police emergency number there. Identify yourself as the terrorist who killed the cops in Wells Church. By now, they'll know what you're talking about. Then I want you to tell the officer who answers three things. Tell him you are leaving the house. Tell him there is a wounded American inside the house who badly needs medical attention. Then say you have planted bombs on houses throughout the block set to go off at 4:35 A.M. Got that?"

"But I told you 4:30—"

"I want you to lie to them—just for me, okay? Can you remember all that?"

"No," the man said nervously. "Not all of it."

"Just dial," Hawker said. "I'll remind you as you go."

The terrorist spoke too quickly into the phone at first. Hawker could tell the officer on duty interrupted to make him slow down. The vigilante had to prompt him only once— about what time the bombs were to go off—a necessary lie to make sure the cops evacuated the entire block without wasting time to look for the bombs. Five minutes could make all the difference.

Hawker didn't want them to find the two actual bombs. Not now.

The desk officer tried to keep the terrorist talking, but Hawker motioned to him to hang up the phone. When he did the vigilante fished a big roll of electrician's tape from his satchel and secured the hands of the first two men behind their backs, then he taped their mouths closed. The man in the middle, the one who had done most of the talking, he left unbound.

"Let's go," Hawker said, waving the Commando at them. "Down the hall and out the back way."

The vigilante stopped them at the master bedroom.

He forced them up against the wall, then he knelt over the wounded American. He was glad to see the wounded man's eyes crack open.

"Hey," Hawker said softly, "you're going to be okay. You're going to make it."

"My kids," he gasped. "Are they . . . are they—"

"Your wife and your kids are fine. Honest." Hawker slid pillows under his legs and pulled a blanket off the bed to cover him as he spoke. "Help's going to be here for you any minute—can you hear the sirens? It's an ambulance on its way. Hang on. Don't die. You have too much to live for."

The wounded man smiled slightly, closed his eyes, and nodded. "Too mean to die," he whispered. "My kids are alive?"

"You'll see them tomorrow. I promise."

Hawker patted the man on the shoulder, then shoved the terrorists on down the hall.

They exited through the broken bedroom window. The three terrorists walked past the corpses of their dead brethren without a sound. Hawker made the terrorist leader take the first bomb. They found the second bomb attached to the side of the house, and Hawker made him carry that one too.

As the vigilante shoved them one by one over the first fence, police cars came screeching around the corner. Hawker noted that their reaction time wasn't all that good—probably eight minutes or so from when the dead cops failed to check in or respond.

Reaction time was never good after midnight on a week-end night.

He knew the EMTs, at least, wouldn't be far behind.

At a brush-covered area between the fences, a hundred yards from any house, the vigilante stopped them. Touching the barrel of the Colt Commando to the temple of the terrorist leader, he said, "Put the bombs on the ground and turn around."

"What are you going to do? You're not going to shoot us—"

"I'm not going to shoot you."

"You are telling the truth?"

"I'm known far and wide for my honesty. Now put your hands behind your back."

Hawker taped the leader's hands heavily, then made them all sit on the ground. He taped the three men together at the neck, so their heads were touching, back-to-back.

"Why are you doing this?"

"Because I'm going to ask you a question, and I want you to answer me honestly."

"Anything! Just don't kill me."

"I've never shot a helpless man in my life. Now answer this question. What country are you from?"

The man gulped and hesitated too long. Hawker nudged him roughly. "What country?"

"I am an Iraqi!"

"Iraq? Why is it I think you're lying?"

"I fight for the freedom of the Iraqi peoples!"

"You fight because you don't have the brains of a radish. Where do you store your ordnance? In the Iraqi Embassy?"

". . . Yes."

"Who's your ambassador?"

The terrorist said a name.

"Then why is it you called a man on the telephone named Isfahan?"

"It . . . that is a code name for him."

"Who is your religious leader?"

"The great and holy Mohammed, merchant of Mecca, prophet of Allah, the savior of mankind, and the one true god."

"Do you really believe that?"

"Yes!"

"Then you're really going to enjoy what's going to happen next."

As the terrorist struggled vainly, Hawker taped his mouth closed, then used a length of rope to tie the legs of the three men together. Using the last of the tape, he secured one bomb to the face of the terrorist leader, then placed the second bomb at his feet.

Hawker stood, straightened his watch cap, and checked his watch. It was 4:02 A.M. Out on the street, police bullhorns boomed: *All residents must evacuate the area immediately. If you do not leave immediately, you may be killed . . ."*

A medical unit was just pulling away, red lights blazing.

The vigilante was satisfied with the way his plan had worked. The black-haired woman and her kids would already be safely out of the area, and now her wounded husband was on his way to the hospital. Because the police had a deadline, they wouldn't have enough manpower to waste time surrounding the area. They would need every available man to help evacuate the area. And in the rush of traffic, they would never notice his escaping in his rental Ford.

Now, there was only the decision of whether to actually

leave the terrorists to the irony of being killed by their own bombs.

It wasn't a difficult decision to make.

As Hawker climbed over the next fence, he called down to the terrorist leader. "Hey—when you see Mohammed, merchant of Mecca, give him my regards, would you?"

THIRTEEN

"The Iraqis are behind the terrorist bombings that have killed seven families in the Washington area in the last eight weeks."

James Hawker sat in a Jacuzzi in his posh hotel suite, hot water sudsing around his neck, a cold bottle of Tüborg in his left hand, the telephone in his right. The Jacuzzi was in a room walled with mirrors, and he saluted himself with the beer as he spoke.

"The Iraqis?" echoed the voice of Agent Lester Rehfuss. "It can't be the Iraqis. Not the Iraqi Embassy, anyway."

"What do you mean, 'It can't be'?"

"Because it can't be the Iraqi Embassy, that's why."

Feeling a sinking feeling in his stomach, Hawker sank lower into the tub. "That's what the guy told me, Lester. He told me he was fighting for the freedom of the Iraqi people."

"The freedom of the Iraqi people, huh?"

"Yeah. The guy had a real way with words."

"Are you sure he wasn't lying?"

"How in the hell could I be sure of that? Do I look like a

mind reader to you? Anyway, why are you so sure these bastards aren't working out of the Iraqi Embassy?"

"Because we've had all the Mideastern embassies watched. Last night the terrorists were traveling in a stolen truck they had painted like a laundry delivery truck. And no such truck entered or exited the Iraqi Embassy."

"Yeah? At what embassy was it seen?"

"At no embassy. There were no suspicious comings or goings from any of the embassies last night or the night before that. Of course, there are thousands of embassy employees in this town. They could be working out of a private residence. We can't watch them all."

"I'm starting to feel frustrated, Lester. And when I get frustrated, I get mad."

"Maybe you're spending too much time looking through that telescope of yours. By the way, how was that asteroid shower you were supposedly tracking?"

Sitting in the Jacuzzi, James Hawker remembered how he had driven safely away from the block where he had confronted the terrorists. He had returned to the park and set up his telescope once again. Then he inserted the low-power eyepiece and focused on the area of dark sky just above the trees to the west. At 4:30 A.M. the rim of sky turned a brilliant pulsating white, then orange, then yellow. The rumble that followed shook the earth and made the leaves of the trees rustle.

"The asteroid shower," said Hawker, "was well worth the wait. It was great."

"Yeah? Well, you're among the very few who thinks so. I

hate to say it, James-boy, but not everyone appreciates what you did last night."

Hawker sat up stiffly in the whirlpool. *"What?"*

"You heard me. You committed the unpardonable crime of making sure the hostages lived. All of them—the woman, both children, and the husband too—"

"The husband? Hey, that's good news. He's going to make it, huh?"

"Looks like it. He's in intensive care in guarded condition, but the prognosis is positive. But that's not the point, Hawk. The point is, all four of those people saw you. The whole family can identify you. It's not . . . healthy—for any of us."

"What the hell did you want me to do? Waste the terrorists *and* the hostages?"

"Jesus, Hawk, don't get mad at me! I'm just saying that the cops know there was an outsider involved. They know someone wasted the terrorists, and they know someone saved the hostages. It's natural for the world to want to know who. Did you see the front page of *The Washington Post?*"

"I subscribed to the *Post* once—but I canceled the subscription when the puppy got old enough to go outside."

"Cute. But listen to the banner headline on page one of the afternoon edition. 'Bombers Foiled By Blond-haired Vigilante.' How's that for accuracy?"

"Jesus, I told the lady not to mention that I helped. Why would she do such a thing?"

"Probably figures you're the Lone Ranger type—you know, too shy to accept the praise you so richly deserve."

"Damn it, I made her promise."

"The woman was half crazy with fear and shock, Hawk. You can't hold her to any promises. Anyway, she or the *Post* got your hair color wrong."

"I'll give you odds on the *Post*."

Rehfuss chuckled. "She told the reporter that seeing you come through her window was like seeing John Wayne arrive."

"The Duke would roll over in his grave."

"Yeah, you're right about that. On their op/ed radio show an hour or so ago, they got one of their ladies to hammer out an editorial on the dangers of vigilante action. She called you a murderer and a Nazi. She said you were more dangerous than the people doing the bombing."

"Good old *Washington Post*—ever the stronghold of limousine liberals and socialist assholes. Does anyone take those people seriously?"

"Yeah—their parents out on Martha's Vineyard and Long Island. I hear they make the maids keep scrapbooks."

Hawker laughed sourly. "So tell me, oh, wise government agent, if the Iraqis are not behind the bombing, who is?"

"That's another reason the police are mad at the mysterious Mister X—you didn't let them take any of the terrorists alive. How in the hell you freed those hostages, killed all the bombers, and still escaped without getting nabbed by the cops is one hell of a trick. And you'd better be glad you pulled it off. Talk is, they think they could have gotten some information if one of the camel jockeys had lived. Did any of them live, Hawk?"

"Yeah, they're singing and dancing right now with some guy named Mohammed, merchant of Mecca."

"Does that mean you killed them all?"

"It does."

"How many were there? I know they found two corpses out behind the house, but after that explosion—"

"There were five of them in all. I took the last three to a brushy area, tied them together, then taped the bombs to them. I guess they sat there for about twenty minutes before the bombs finally went off—an unpleasant wait, I'd think."

Rehfuss whistled softly. "Jesus, you are a *cold* bastard, aren't you? I guess that explains reports of human appendages raining down on the nation's capital."

"Justice is a rare commodity, Lester. I think what they got was just. What about the two corpses I left behind? Did you get any make on them?"

"Nope. Not yet. The Washington P.D. is a good bunch, and if they don't have any luck, they'll turn it over to the FBI. If those boys can't place the fingerprints, it means the dearly departed not only entered this country illegally, but they probably wore gloves the whole time they were here."

"I hope they hurry. I have the feeling those five weren't acting alone. And whoever is behind it isn't going to be happy about losing a whole crew. I think they'll plan another bombing real soon."

"So what's your next move, Hawk?"

"I have to get some scribbling on an appointment calendar translated."

"What language?"

"Arabic, I think."

"I can have that done for you. Can you drop it off at the complex gatehouse?"

"Sure. I'm going downtown to the Capitol Building anyway. I can stop on the way."

"The Capitol? I can't picture you taking one of those guided tours."

"I'm not. I've got an appointment with Senator Thy Estes."

"Senator Estes!" Rehfuss gave a bawdy whistle. "Consider yourself among the lucky few, Hawk. A lot of very wealthy, very important men would like to have a private appointment with that lady."

"She's pretty?"

"The word 'pretty' doesn't cover it. She's got that weird magnetism . . . I don't know what it is or what you would call it, but it makes her attractive and desirable as hell. I'm not the only one who has noticed it. Hell, she's no spring chicken. She must be in her mid-forties, but she's got that bright red hair, and that body—but you don't need to hear any more. You'll see for yourself. But remember, she's a married lady."

"The Senator's First Gentleman, huh?"

"Not exactly. Her husband is one of the biggest assholes in D.C.—a real estate baron who has a reputation for being a twenty-four-hour drunk. The really mean gossip has it that he likes to play weird games with male hookers when the mood is upon him. But the senator is a straight arrow, a really great lady who deserves a hell of a lot better."

"I just want to see if she knows any more about her sister's family getting blown up. I could care less about the honorable senator's marriage history or what she looks like."

"Okay, okay—I was just trying to fill you in."

"I appreciate it, ole friend, and I've got one more question."

"Yeah?"

"You know anything about a man called Isfahan?"

There was a short silence on the other end of the phone. "Doesn't ring a bell, but I can sure check around. Where did you hear it?"

"From the terrorists—just before I cast their fates to the wind."

"You *are* a cold bastard."

"Yeah, but I'm lovable. Talk to you later, Lester—"

"Wait a minute, Hawk."

"Yeah?"

"Well . . . I just wanted to tell you that not everyone thinks you screwed up last night. I, for one, think you did a hell of a job. Admiral Percival agrees. He told me to give you his compliments."

"Lester?"

"Yes?"

"Tell him I'd prefer the half-million dollars."

FOURTEEN

James Hawker had entered the Capitol Building by the west portico after first standing on the steps near the crypt, reviewing in silence the Statue of Freedom perched atop the building's bright white cupola.

Then he made his way down the marble halls of the north wing, the Senate side of the Capitol, along the line of open doors. Most of the senators weren't in their offices. But their secretaries were. Hawker took an informal survey as he walked. He saw more than two dozen secretaries between the rotunda and Thy Estes's office. All of them were very pretty. Most of them were brunettes or blondes. They looked up and smiled as Hawker *clickity-clacked* by. They were firm-breasted, sleek, stylish, and had bodies that squeezed at the heart.

Hawker had seen these women before on his few previous trips to Washington, and though the faces changed, the personality type did not. These were the power groupies, the best of the large female herd attracted to D.C. by the allure of association with the men who held the reins of history.

They came in many guises, in many roles. In the 1960s they had come as peace advocates or freedom marchers. Now the favorite facade was that of the "modern" woman, an independent business person who demanded respect and equality. But whatever the current social costume happened to be, the goals of the power groupies remained always the same: do anything they had to do to find some niche in the power structure, then hang on to that little crevice of importance by whatever means necessary.

The standard vehicle was, of course, sex. As a result, the prettiest of the power groupies usually prevailed. The rest either meshed into the Washington treadmill of lesser jobs, or they went home with the hopes of marrying a member of the hometown power structure. Some, no doubt, succeeded at neither, and these girls were to be found beneath the streetlamps in the bowels of the city.

In truth the jobs of the successful and unsuccessful did not differ all that much.

Hawker's appointment with Senator Thy Estes was scheduled to last twenty minutes. It was on her secretary's agenda: "James Hawker, friend of J. M. Hayes: 5:10 P.M. to 5:30."

It was to have been the senator's last appointment of the day, a courtesy call that demanded her to do nothing more than shake hands and smile.

As it turned out, though, she and Hawker were still talking when the senator's brass and maple grandmother clock gonged seven times.

Her secretary had long gone, as had most of the other workers in the north wing of the Capitol Building.

To Hawker it seemed like they had just started talking. As in the film musicals of old, time flew by. Lester Rehfuss was right. The woman had a weird magnetism. It had nothing to do with her looks—although she was attractive enough. She was a solid-looking woman in her early forties, two inches under six feet, with good shoulders, long runner's legs, firm globes of buttocks beneath the gray tweed skirt suit she wore. Her heavy breasts, like well-formed melons, strained against her prim white blouse. She had glistening mahogany hair that she wore up in a matronly bun, and Hawker guessed it added a year or two to her looks. But her face had a sly, ripe handsomeness, a polished-wood sort of beauty, like Maureen O'Hara, and there was something in her jade-green eyes that glimmered with challenge—something untouchable, unknowable, but exciting. It was with her eyes that she seemed to communicate most effectively. Her lips formed sentences: sometimes interesting, sometimes funny, always articulate. But her eyes spoke of intimacy: an intellectual intimacy that was sometimes underscored by the suggestion of a warmer, more physical variety of closeness.

As Hawker sat talking to her, he tried to sort it out on some deeper level.

It wasn't easy to understand. Within five minutes of meeting the woman she had made him feel like the wisest, funniest, most important man in her life. Her intense interest in his every word took Hawker aback at first. But then he realized that she was one of the very few people who had the energy or the ability to make people feel instantly good about themselves, immediately of greater worth than allotted them by the drab world outside. Hawker understood that it was exactly for this reason that she was a United States senator. People who met her felt the magnetism; they felt her intense interest in them; they trusted her and they damn well voted for her.

It was with a slight twinge of jealousy that the vigilante realized that *all* men who had sat across the desk from her felt as she had made him feel. And it irritated him that he would react emotionally to a political technique. She was just a woman, damn it, just another politician. She was married besides, and even if she wasn't, it would be unlikely that a female U.S. senator would allow herself to get romantically involved with a man who wasn't part of the power structure and, worse, refused to be a cog in anyone's machine.

Or would she?

It irritated Hawker even more that he cared.

He sat in a heavy leather chair across the desk from her. The desk was a huge polished oval of mahogany. On it was a pale leather blotter, neat baskets of correspondence, a brass nameplate, and a quill pen in an inkwell. In one corner of the room was the American flag; in the other corner, the flag of the state that had elected her. On the wall were photographs of her with the President and with various other world leaders.

They had spent the first hour in fast and easy, often humorous conversation about subjects that seemed to link together in a chain. He had gotten his tan in Florida? She loved Florida, yes, especially the west coast. He must know a great deal about fishing. She loved to fish for tarpon, but could he *really* teach her how to use a fly rod well enough to take a fish that size? And so the conversation went. From fishing to boats to Key West to Lake Michigan to their mutual friend Jacob Montgomery Hayes, to Chicago to great vacation spots to Little Cayman Island. Hawker was so captivated by her curious blend of girlishness, beauty, intellect, sexuality, and maturity that he had to keep reminding himself that this wasn't just a woman he was talking to, this was a well-rehearsed, well-schooled package known as a United States senator. She was no more attracted to him than she was the average friend-of-a-friend from off the street.

Finally embarrassed by his own schoolboy emotion, Hawker forced himself to turn abruptly businesslike.

"Senator Estes," he said, "I know you're a busy person, so maybe I'd better ask my questions and let you get about your business."

The woman leaned back in her chair, her eyebrows raised. "Jake Hayes said you had a one-track mind when it came to your . . . profession. So far, everything he's told me about you has proven true."

"Oh?"

"Yes—and it's all good, by the way." She smiled. "Why do you look at me like that? It's because you're surprised Jake would talk to anybody about you, isn't it? Don't worry, James. Jake and I are very old and very dear friends. I've been hearing about you ever since that . . . that terrible night when his son was murdered. Since then, I have heard a great deal about James Hawker. He's awfully fond of you, you know. He says you're one of the great anachronisms. He says you're really from another time, a time of quests and knights and ladies fair. But you probably know Jake's penchant for mysticism—reincarnation and such things. I must say, though, he painted an awfully attractive picture of you."

"That was kind of Jacob, Senator Estes, but right now I think we ought to discuss the reason I am here."

"Certainly, James, but I'm in no hurry. Really. And, please call me Thy—as in *the*ater, remember." She settled back over the desk, smiling.

"Okay . . . Thy. It may be painful for you to talk about so soon, but I'd like to know more about your late sister, Betty Rutledge, and her family."

The smile slowly gave way to a look of resignation. "I'll help you in any way I can."

Hawker nodded, sorry that he had stripped away her energized facade with one chilling sentence. "I'm not even sure what I want to know, Thy," he began. "Anything might help. The little things can sometimes be pieced together to make a very important chunk of the puzzle. I guess what I'm looking for is some clue to explain why your sister's home was chosen out of all the houses in Bethesda to be bombed."

"But the bombings are random, aren't they, James? That's what everyone says."

"Maybe they are, Thy. But I get real uncomfortable when people start connecting coincidence with premeditated murder. It's a damn rare combination. It's possible, sure—maybe even probable in this case. Terrorists motivated by a political or religious cause seldom go by the book. But before I accept the killings as random, I need to prove it to myself. It seems very unlikely that the terrorists would murder more than two dozen people in seven different attacks without knowing at least a few of the victims."

The senator thought for a moment. "When you put it that

way, James, it makes sense. It's hard to believe that they would kill that many people without grinding a few personal axes." She looked at him pointedly. "What about last night in Wells Church? Was *that* random? Or had they already picked out their victims?"

Hawker returned her level gaze. "Last night? How would I know? All I know is what I read in the papers, Senator."

"I see. Is that the way you want it, James?"

"I'm afraid that's the way it has to be."

"I don't know why, but you make one anxious to be taken into your confidence, anxious to earn some demonstration of your respect. I'm sorry I don't yet qualify. But, if the day did come when you felt you could trust me, I would be very pleased to listen."

Her green eyes were earnest, her face handsomer for its seriousness, and once again Hawker felt the schoolboy rush of emotion. What did they used to call it? Smitten. That's right, he was smitten. He wanted to take the woman in his arms and hold her close and treat her as kindly as one human being can treat another.

Instead, he shrugged with cold indifference. "I'm still waiting to hear about your late sister's family."

"I don't really even know how to begin."

"How about with the fact that you are the only woman on the Senate Foreign Relations Committee. Do you think there's any chance of a connection? Maybe the terrorists were trying to hurt you by bombing your sister's house."

"God, I'd never even thought about that—"

"And you don't need to think about it unless the terrorists

have let you know that you are the reason. To hurt you, they would have to inform you. How about it, Senator Estes? Any cryptic notes or anonymous calls?"

The woman thought for a moment. "No-o-o-o. Nothing that I would consider suspicious."

"Any important hearings coming up that might fare better if you weren't at full emotional strength?"

"That would be a possibility at almost any other time of the year—but not now. You see, we're getting ready for a short spring recess."

"Have you made any enemies in the Mideastern diplomatic corps?"

"Who can say what those people think? They all smile like stray dogs. But I think that I am on reasonably good terms with most of them."

Hawker scowled at the wall.

"I'm afraid I'm not helping much," the woman smiled, getting up from her desk. She came around the corner and touched Hawker's arm gently. The vigilante drew his arm away at the heat of her touch, and the woman smiled at him as she might at a teenager who had stumbled over his feet. "Why don't we continue this conversation over dinner?" she suggested.

"I'm afraid I already have plans," Hawker heard himself say—and immediately hated himself for telling such a stupid lie.

"Oh? Oh. I see." The smile brightened. "Well, you can at least walk me to my car then. We can talk more on the way."

"I'd be happy to, Senator—"

"It's *Thy*, damn it!"

FIFTEEN

The man confronted them in the back parking lot, a huge balding man with pale-pink skin and bowling-ball fists. He weaved toward them, his expensive suit wrinkled, tie loosened, slurring his words and scowling like a man with murder on his mind.

Thy Estes stopped cold when she saw him, then pulled instinctively closer to Hawker.

"So where is the snooty bitch off to tonight?" the man roared, charging closer. "The Far East? The White House? Or maybe just that red-haired asshole's bed."

Hawker looked quickly at the woman beside him. Her face had gone stern, pale, fearful.

"Didn't even return my calls . . . damn secretary told me you were out of the office—"

"I was out of the office, Jack!"

"Lying bitch!"

The big man grabbed her wrist with his right hand and tried to push Hawker roughly aside with his shoulder. The vigilante stomped down hard on the arch of his foot and grabbed him by the lapels when he opened his mouth to roar in pain.

"I don't know who you are, friend, but I think you ought to go crawl in a corner and sleep it off."

The big man took a lumbering swing at Hawker. The vigilante ducked under it, then stepped away from a ponderous left hook. Hawker shoved him roughly away. "Friend, even drunks can go too far. Now I'll give you one last warning—"

The man threw himself at Hawker, catching him with a painful right to the side of the neck. Hawker's face flushed. He drove his left hand deep into the man's soft belly, then hit him with a halfhearted punch to the jaw. The big man backpedaled and fell to the asphalt, out cold.

"Jesus," said Hawker in disbelief, "I didn't even hit him hard."

The woman said nothing and walked quickly to the side of the fallen man. She knelt over him and checked his pulse, then drew open an eyelid to check his pupils.

She stood abruptly. Her face was red, half anger, half pain. "Let's go," she snapped.

"But, Senator, we can't just leave him—"

"Please, James, let's go. *Now.*"

The vigilante shrugged and walked her quickly toward the line of parked cars.

"Which one is yours?"

"I'm not taking my car," she said, almost whispering.

"What?"

"I'm going with you, James. Please. Please don't ask me to explain." She looked at him, green eyes flashing. "And please don't repeat that phony line about your having another appointment."

"Yes, ma'am!"

"Something you will learn very quickly about me is that I have an uncanny knack for reading people. Our friend Jake Hayes says it's because I'm parapsychic. I prefer to think I have a built-in bullshit detector."

"Yes, ma'am."

"And quit calling me, 'ma'am'!"

"Yes . . . *Thy!*"

"Then let's go."

"And just leave that jerk back there unconscious?"

The woman shook herself, furious. "In the first place, he's not unconscious—I looked at his eyes, remember? He's playing possum. He's a coward." She looked up at the vigilante, her face still red and her eyes still glittering, and slid her arm beneath his. "In the second place, Mr. Hawker, he can drive my car home when he sobers up. You see, that jerk is my husband."

Hawker had driven them along Constitution Avenue, past the statue of Grant, past the Smithsonian Institution, then north on Ninth Street, past Ford's Theatre, where the curtain rang down on Abraham Lincoln. The woman directed him as he drove, and they ended up at a tiny Greek restaurant drinking ouzo, eating stuffed grape leaves and lamb, and talking unreservedly.

She had spoken with subdued emotion about her husband's drinking problem, how she felt partially to blame for it, that they were unable to have children, how their marriage had crumbled, why they now stayed together for the sake of appearances. Then she had turned to another unhappy subject—the death of her sister and her sister's family. Her stories were filled with obvious affection, sometimes humor, and, finally, tears.

Hawker had listened sympathetically, saying little, letting the emotion drain out of her at its own pace. As he listened, he sipped at the clear, anise-flavored ouzo, which, when poured over ice, turned a milky white. Ouzo was one of the more devastating liqueurs in the world, and the vigilante was careful not to drink it too quickly. The senator, he noticed, was not being quite as careful. He made no effort to caution her. She was no fool, and she certainly wasn't naive. She knew exactly what she was doing.

"And that's the story of my dear sister and her lovely family," Thy Estes said, wiping her eyes and fighting back a case of the sniffles. "Now there's only poor young Luke left—for some reason, he was out on the street when the bomb went off. And I'm not so sure he wouldn't have been better off if he had been inside. He saw what the bomb did to his family. He saw the wreckage and the bits and pieces of his father and sisters and baby brother. They put him in a psychiatric ward, you know. The dear child won't say any word but 'Daddy'—not even to me. He just stares off into space. And he is such a damn bright boy!"

"They must have loved each other very much," Hawker put in softly.

"They were an extremely close family. And do you know what troubles me more than anything? I talked to Betty on the telephone the night before they were killed. She seemed very upset about something. Finally, she told me Luke and her husband had had a very bitter argument. Something about her husband backing down from three students in a fight, and embarrassing Luke—" Hawker suddenly straightened in his chair, now very interested in what the woman was saying. "I so wish Luke and Chester hadn't had that fight. I'm sure Luke must be thinking about it now and feeling guilty—"

"What kind of students?" Hawker interrupted. "Why would three students challenge a grown man to a fight?"

The senator looked confused for a moment. "College students, I guess. Apparently they ran a stop sign and did some minor damage to Chester's car. But that's not the point, James—"

"Maybe not, Thy, but I'd like to hear more about it. Give me all the details you have."

The woman shrugged, poured herself an inch of ouzo in a whiskey tumbler, and said, "I guess the accident happened the day I called, a Thursday. No one was hurt, but the students refused to stay at the scene until the police came. Chester, of course, insisted that they stay. The students became very abusive, swearing at him and calling him all kinds of foul names. Luke was there, and he apparently lost his temper. He wanted to fight the three college guys, but his dad held him back. That night, I guess they argued, and Lukie called his dad a coward. Betty was very upset, of course. Luke and Chester were normally very close."

"Thy, don't people usually exchange telephone numbers and addresses when they've had an accident?"

"Yes, I guess so, James. But these three students skipped,

as I said. Besides, Betty said something about Chester having a tough time communicating with them because they were foreigners—"

"Foreigners? From what country, Thy?"

The woman shook her head slowly. "You know, James, I've finally realized why you're so interested. God, I am dense sometimes. I don't know where the students were from, Betty didn't say. Chester *did* get their license number before they drove off, but I don't know what the number was of course. Do you really think there might be some connection?"

Hawker shrugged. "I told you how I felt about coincidence. Don't you think it's probable that Chester called their license number in to the police?"

"Chester was a meticulous man. I'm sure he would have notified the police."

"Don't you think it's possible that Chester also gave the students his telephone number, hoping they would have their insurance company contact him?"

The woman gestured with her palms upward. "I really couldn't say. I just know the three students were very abusive. Betty said they called him horrible names. He ignored the things they said. Lukie couldn't, and I guess it hurt him to see his father so humiliated."

Hawker stood up quickly. "I need to get back to my hotel room, Thy. I need to check something. It's important. Can I drop you at your home?"

The pretty woman stood, touching the table as if to steady herself. "That last glass of ouzo put my head to spinning," she said smiling, ". . . and, no, you can't drop me at home. I really don't care to fight with my husband tonight. You can take me back to the Capitol, if you like—they have rooms for us there. Lately, I've been calling the office home." Her green eyes grew sharp, glistening. "Or, if you think you could use my help, I'd be happy to come back to your hotel room."

Hawker dropped three tens and a five onto the check tray and took her arm. "The Capitol it is, Senator . . ."

SIXTEEN

Alone in his hotel suite, James Hawker sat looking intently at the screen of his Apple III computer. He had booted it with the Modem 1200 software and flicked on the modem unit, which had been jacked into the telephone line. He reset the configuration parameters and entered the two telephone numbers given to him by Lester Rehfuss. One of the numbers was for the National Crime Information Center (NCIC), the other for the D.C. Police Department's computer center.

That done, he slid the ingenious but illegal RUSTLED software into the second disk drive. RUSTLED (Random Ultraspeed Taps on Locked Entry Data) had been conceived and programmed by a friend of his. Using a brilliant system of probability, it tried and retried various ID numbers and passwords until it broke through a computer's security system. Using RUSTLED, Hawker could tap into almost any high-security computer bank in the world.

Finally the vigilante switched to the terminal mode. From the modem's speaker he could hear the number of NCIC being dialed. Since NCIC was an open information data system, RUS-TLED wouldn't be needed. When the menu flashed on the screen, Hawker indicated the D.C. area, then indicated "vehicular."

The screen began to roll a seemingly endless list of stolen cars, names of wanted car thieves, descriptions of cars involved in hit-and-runs. Hawker watched the hit-and-runs carefully, but found nothing that mentioned Chester Rutledge. He wasn't surprised. A fender-bender hit-and-run wasn't likely to make NCIC, but since it was the easiest to get into, Hawker had tried it first.

He returned to the computer's phone director and selected the number to the more confidential Washington P.D. data system. The modem dialed it and Hawker watched the screen for a few minutes as RUSTLED offered a name, was cut off by the security system, then dialed again and tried another.

It might take a while.

Hawker got up and cracked a cold bottle of Strohs, stripped off his clothes, and settled down into the hot tub. He tried to concentrate on what he would do if he found the names of the three students, but his mind kept wandering. He kept thinking about Senator Thy Estes, wondering what magic she possessed to capture him so swiftly. Had she really offered herself to him, or was it just part of the politician's facade? She had offered to come back to his hotel room—but was it anything more than a polite gesture?

For some reason, Hawker couldn't let himself believe it was.

He pictured her alone in her room in the Capitol Building. What would she be doing right now? Reading, probably. Maybe working late in her office. Hawker's imagination took over, and he found himself trying to picture her naked, the dark mahogany hair hanging down, her face, like polished wood, looking up into his. It was with some surprise that Hawker realized he had never bedded a woman older than himself. But a United States senator? Hawker had no interest in public women. Fashion models, actresses, dancers—he had known his share, and they were all a disappointment. Still, the image of Thy Estes naked, with her dark hair hanging down lingered in his mind . . .

The soft chime of the computer yanked his attention back to reality.

RUSTLED had broken the code. His computer was now linked to the data banks of the Washington Police Department.

Hawker dried himself quickly, pulled on his clothes, and seated himself at the computer. Once again, he maneuvered through the computer's menu, zeroing in on the information he needed.

This time, he did not come up empty-handed:

#141769 . . . complainant Chester A. Rutledge/1212 Kenwood/Bethesda, MD/'84 Olds Cutlass, Lic. VJ431J; Est. Damage: $800. Hit-run charges pending on driver of '85 Lincoln Mk.4 Blk 4-door, Lic. Diplomatic Service 117, registered to Hon. Isfahan Shiraz/(Tehran, Iran)/U.S.: 2007 Bleaker/Fairmoor Heights, D.C. Warrant issued 5-14-85.

Isfahan!

With a coldly steady hand, Hawker noted the information on a slip of paper and immediately began dressing himself. To bang into the name of Isfahan twice was no coincidence. There was no doubt in his mind now about who was behind the deadly series of bombings that had killed so many people. Now it did not matter what the dead Syrian's, Rultan's, appointment calendar said. Nor did he need the investigative resources of Lester Rehfuss or the CIA or the FBI or any other agency.

Now it was all too clear. He knew what country was behind the carnage—Iran—and he knew that a diplomat named Isfahan Shiraz was involved with the bombings. Hawker also knew that three of Isfahan's goons, three foreign students, had vaporized the family of Chester A. Rutledge because he had exchanged insults with them after a minor traffic accident.

How many others were involved? There was no way of knowing. But one thing was for sure: tonight, he would find out. And he would bring the Iranian bastards to their knees.

Hawker checked his watch. It was only 10:23 P.M. The ideal time to attempt his break-in would be after 3 A.M. He had a hell of a lot of time to waste before he could drive to 2007 Bleaker in Fairmoor Heights.

Sleep was impossible. Hawker toyed with the idea of calling Thy Estes, but shrugged it off as bad judgment. But while selecting his weaponry, a way to waste the time was provided for him.

The phone rang.

It was Thy Estes.

In an alto voice that was softer than he remembered it, she said, "I don't want to sound brazen, James, but I could use a friend right now. Interested?"

"My place or yours, Senator?"

Her laughter was good to hear. "How about *our* place, citizen—your taxes helped pay for the Capitol too."

SEVENTEEN

"I'm glad you could come, James. It's funny, but out of all the people I know, there are very, very few I can talk to intimately. You see, a senator is supposed to solve problems, not share them. People get nervous when they see a chink in the armor. You're not that kind of person, James. Are you?"

Once again, Hawker stood in front of the vast oval desk. Thy Estes sat in the great leather chair, her fingers interlocked, drumming among themselves with a nervousness that did not show on her face.

"We all have our weak days, Thy. Even senators. Why should it bother me?"

The woman unlocked her hands, took off her amber-rimmed glasses, and remounted them on her head, like ski goggles. She now wore pale green warm-up silks. The jacket was not zipped, and the burnt-orange body stocking was taut over the mature swell of her breasts. There was a light scent in the air, a mixture of shampoo and soap and, fainter yet, body musk. Hawker guessed she had been working out before he arrived.

"Would you like a drink, James?"

"I'd like a beer."

She stood and motioned him through a door at the back of the office. Hands in his pockets, Hawker followed her into a room about the size of the office. The floor was plushly carpeted and there were heavy drapes that were to give the impression of a window—but there was no window. On the near wall was a couch already pulled out into a bed. Opposite it was a multitiered electronics station that held three television sets, a stereo system, a personal computer, an intercom, and two telephones.

"My private chambers," she said, stepping behind the portable bar. "Judging from the carpet and curtains, the senator here before me must have been in love with Holiday Inns. I keep planning to have it redone, but I never seem to find the time." She opened the door of the small refrigerator. "What kind of beer do you like?"

"Any kind but Pearl Light."

She smiled and handed him a steaming bottle of Becks. "I won't tell my honorable colleagues from Texas you said that. And I guess I'll have . . . let's see, a good stiff scotch and soda."

"Still upset about your husband, senator?"

Ice clinked in the heavy bar glass as she looked up at him. "No. The relationship with my husband ended long ago, even before I was elected to this fair office. I guess I didn't divorce him then because I didn't want it to hurt my political career. Pretty selfish, huh? I don't divorce him now because I don't want our private lives dragged through the mud by the newspapers."

"Then you're upset about something else?"

She took a long gulp of scotch, then seemed to sag a little as the alcohol moved through her body. "Yes, James, I am upset about something. I'm upset about . . . about you."

"Me?"

"Yes, you!" She put the glass down on the bar and leaned toward him. "Tell me one thing. Why don't you like me?"

"Like you? Thy, I like you very much—"

"Then why did you spend the whole early evening giving me the cold shoulder?"

Hawker actually stuttered in surprise. "I did . . . didn't give you a cold anything—"

"Don't forget about my built-in bullshit detector, Mr. James Hawker. You got your ten-foot pole out and held me at bay the entire time!" Both hands were on the bar now, and she leaned across glowering at him, half in jest but half serious too. "What's the matter with me? Are my eyes too dark? Too bright? Am I too tall, too short? Or maybe I'm too old, is that it? I'm only forty-three for Christ's sake. *Geeze!*" She jammed her hands on her hips and turned slightly away from him, refusing to meet his eyes. "After all that I had heard about you from Jake Hayes, I was really anxious to meet you, like a girl excited about a big date. I spent half an hour last night picking out just the right clothes, just the right way to wear my hair. I wanted to seem professional, but not stodgy; I wanted to look attractive but not cheap. That first hour with you was wonderful. It was so good to actually have a *conversation* with someone. You liked me! I *know* you liked me. But then, for god knows what reason, you started acting like I had spinach between my teeth. Why? I forced down three of those damn ouzos to get my courage up, and then I practically insisted you take me to your hotel." She looked at him once more. "And you turned me down you . . . you . . . *Republican!*"

Hawker began to laugh. It began as a low cough, and when he could hold it no longer, the laughter became a long, rolling peal. "God," he gasped, rubbing his eyes, "what an idiot I've been!"

"Don't expect me to contradict you!"

"But don't you see? It was because . . . because . . ." Hawker broke down in another chorus of laughter.

"Why, damn it? Why?"

Hawker stood, took the woman's hand, and hugged her. "Take me for a walk, woman. Show me around this mansion of yours—but get me out of here or I won't be able to stop laughing."

Steering him by the hand, smiling like a schoolgirl, Thy Estes led Hawker down the long marble halls of the Capitol. They walked past the empty committee rooms, restaurants, through the Hall of Columns. At a massive double door she stopped and said to a uniformed guard, "Hi, Jack! I'm showing a friend of mine around tonight. Mind if we go in?"

The guard grinned, happy to be called by name. "Sure thing, Senator Estes. Go right ahead. Anything else I can do for you?"

"Not a thing, Jack. We'll probably go out through the back way, so don't worry about us. Good night!"

They stepped into a basin of a room, built in tiers with aged, ornate wood and marble, with plush carpet, flags, and galleries overhead. In the center of the basin, on the lowest floor level, were five massive desks, three in a line and two off to the side, like a pyramid. The room smelled good, like a library.

"Welcome to the chambers of the United States Senate," Thy Estes said grandly. She took Hawker's arm and pulled close. He could feel the heat and weight of her left breast. "Care for a tour?" she asked.

Hawker looked down into her green eyes. They seemed to be burning. There was no mistaking the heavy-lidded, sloe-eyed, flushed expression. "As long as you keep it short, lady," he said. "I'm kind of anxious to get back to your room."

The Senate Chamber was bathed in shadows and soft light. She showed him her seat, the electronic voting mechanism, and pointed out the seats of some of her more famous colleagues. The whole time, Hawker could feel the tension building in his stomach, the butterflies of sexual anticipation. It wouldn't have been so bad, but he could see signs of the same physical wanting in her: the shortness of breath, the nervous movements, the projectile shape of her nipples hardening beneath the body stocking.

"And do you see the two light bulbs beneath the chandelier?" Thy Estes said, now conducting the tour by rote. "The red bulb indicates that an executive session is in progress. The white one indicates a regular session."

They stood now at the front of the Senate well. Separating them from the doorway was a massive podium. Hawker turned and looked deep into the woman's eyes . . .

"And this is the Vice President's seat," she continued. "Here he's called the President of the Senate."

He reached out and unsnapped the barrette in her hair. A mahogany veil swung down onto her shoulders, and she shook her head, so that the hair spread around her face and slightly over one eye . . .

"The Secretary of the Senate—"

Hawker took her by the shoulders and pulled her against him . . .

"—sits to the right of the Vice President—"

Hawker began to kiss her neck, feeling her gasp slightly as he slid the green warm-up jacket off her, then rolled the burnt-orange body stocking down over her shoulders to her waist. Her breasts seemed to expand and settle, relieved to be free, and he lifted them in his hands, squeezing the weight of them softly.

The woman moaned and arched as Hawker kissed her shoulders and chest, then touched his tongue to the long nipple of her right breast. The skin was as translucent as expensive paper, and the white orb was webbed by delicate blue veins. The veins seemed to throb and darken as Hawker sucked on the woman's nipple.

"God, James, you're making me so dizzy—"

"I'll help you put your jacket on, and we'll go back to your room."

"No! God, I can't wait. Please! Don't stop, not yet!"

Without waiting for a reply, the woman dropped to her knees and, with shaking hands, unbuckled Hawker's belt. The vigilante knotted his fingers in her hair as she pulled his pants, then his briefs, down around his ankles.

"My goodness!" she exclaimed softly, taking him in her two small hands.

"Your goodness has nothing to do with it," Hawker moaned.

There was no doubt that Thy Estes enjoyed what she was doing. She made the small hungry noises of an animal as she took him into her mouth and began an assault, with tongue and suction, that seemed to draw at his very soul. When Hawker could stand it no longer, he forced the woman's face away from him. Wordlessly, she lay back on the floor and let the vigilante strip the rest of her clothes away. She was a beautiful woman indeed, with a full mature body that had been well tended. Her hips were wide, moist, and ready. Her pubic hair was a darker, glossier shade of auburn than the hair on her head, and her breasts flattened and spread themselves beneath their own weight. She ran her hands over her body, eyes half closed in ecstasy, as Hawker took off his own clothes and draped them over a huge chair.

"The Vice President's chair," Thy Estes whispered, giggling, as the vigilante knelt before her.

Hawker said nothing as he let the woman roll him over onto the carpet so that now she was on top. She lifted her hips, positioned herself, then forced Hawker to enter her with a long, strong thrust of her hips. "*Oh . . .*" she whispered softly, "yes . . . yes . . . yes . . . harder, please, harder. Make me feel like a woman, James. Make me feel like the most desirable lady in creation . . ."

As the woman found the rhythm she wanted—slow, angled, and hard enough so that her pelvis slapped against his—Hawker took a discreet look at his Seiko Submariner watch.

12:19.

Hawker was relieved to see he had plenty of time.

There was every indication that Senator Thy Estes was about to stage her first filibuster on the Senate floor . . .

EIGHTEEN

At 1:45 A.M., James Hawker, refreshed but weary, content but just a little sore, trotted down the steps of the Capitol Building. The May night was cool, blustery, and ripe with spring thaw. Sporadic traffic echoed through the streets.

His rental Ford was parked beside a line of newspaper dispensers. One of the headlines caught his attention:

"Teen Prom Queen Gunned Down"

Hawker shook his head as he got into the car. Who in the hell would shoot a defenseless teenage girl? It was Them, the nameless, faceless Them, savages who walked the streets, walked the streets of every city in the country.

Maybe tonight he could rid the land of just a few of Them.

Hawker started the car, checked the map under the dome light, and steered off through the glistening streets toward Fairmoor Heights, his jaw set tightly.

Within half an hour he had found 2007 Bleaker, an estate of dark trees and rolling grounds set within a high concrete wall. At the entrance was a massive wrought-iron gate and a small lighted guard's station. Inside the little station two dark, swarthy men sat within smoking, playing cards.

Hawker drove past without slowing.

He had one thing in his favor: the estate was set apart from the other mansions in the area by its own acreage. Once he got in, noise—within reason—wouldn't matter all that much.

Hawker parked in a church parking lot two blocks from the back of the estate. He strapped on the heavy Colt revolver in its shoulder holster, checked the canvas chest-pack to see if it had everything he might need.

Finally, he hefted the little Ingram MAC-11 submachine gun. With the metal stock folded, it was only ten inches long. Unloaded, it weighed less than a pound. Its box clip held thirty-two rounds of nine-mm cartridges, and the silencer he screwed onto the barrel was longer than the weapon. Taped to the strap of the chest-pack were six more full clips.

When he was ready the vigilante pulled on an old trench coat and trotted down the dark sidewalk to the back wall of the estate.

While driving around the block he had pinpointed the telephone terminal. It was a ground terminal, green and tubular, and now he knelt beside it, watching carefully for traffic. At Thy Estes's office he had called Information to see if there was a telephone number for Isfahan Shiraz. As he expected, the number was unlisted. He had toyed with the idea of calling Lester Rehfuss and asking him to get it, but he felt that, if he told Lester what he knew, the CIA might pull him off the case and send its own people.

Now he had to play it by ear. He loosened the single screw

that held the green cap and removed the top of the terminal. Using his little Tekna flashlight, he studied the brass pairs. Candy-colored wires ran to the entire vertical row of them, but only four drop lines were connected. Hawker had no way of knowing if they all led inside to the estate, but it was not unlikely. Shiraz might well have two private lines, and the other two lines might be wired to burglar alarms.

Carefully, Hawker loosened the brass nuts and disconnected all the wires.

When he was done he listened closely for any gong of alarm from the security system Shiraz no doubt employed.

Except for the wind in the trees, there was no sound.

Bundling the old trench coat around him, Hawker walked quickly around the block to the front of the estate. When the wrought-iron gate and the guard station came into view, his walk abruptly changed. He began to weave and stagger, head bowed, hands stuffed in pockets. He began to sing:

"Mamas, don't let your cowboys grow up to be babies . . ."

He sang and staggered up to the gate, fell against it, and slid down to the asphalt still singing.

"Hey! You there! Get away, you drunk! We call the police, have your ass arrested. Hey! You, wake up!"

Hawker groaned and looked up. The two guards, dressed in khaki, stood within the gate. Each of the men held a revolver pointed at his head.

"Oh-h-h," the vigilante moaned, "going to be sick. Got to throw up."

"You no puke your guts here, you bum! Go away now!"

"Leave me alone . . . got to vomit . . ."

Hawker got to his knees and, holding his stomach, began to heave. Immediately, the big gate swung open. From the corner of his eye Hawker watched as the two guards holstered their weapons so they could drag him into the street.

They did not get the chance.

From beneath the trench coat Hawker pulled the Ingram submachine gun and shot them both quickly with short bursts. When the Iranians hit the asphalt, it was like the thud of heavy bags of fruit.

Quickly, Hawker jumped to his feet and dragged them both into the bushes inside the estate. He pulled the gate closed behind him and stripped off the trench coat. From the oversized pockets he took his Navy watch cap and a tin of military skin-black. He streaked his face with the grease, then pulled on a pair of thin leather gloves.

It was 2:45 A.M.

He could see the lights of the house through the trees. It was elevated on a hill, down a winding asphalt drive. Hawker trotted down the drive, his New Balance running shoes making almost no noise. The drive ended at a circular commons in front of the house. Hawker stopped. It was a massive brick house, three stories high, with keystone windows and layers of ivy. There were dim lights burning on the bottom floor, and one bright window upstairs. He watched for several minutes, expecting someone to be patrolling outside the house.

No one there.

Cautiously, Hawker made his way to the door—and had the wind knocked out of him by something big, dark, and heavy that hit him from the side.

It was a third guard, the guard he had expected to be there but had not seen.

The man wrestled Hawker to the ground, but the vigilante still held the Ingram. He swung the silencer against the guard's chest and squeezed off another short burst. The impact of the slugs knocked the man off Hawker onto the ground. The guard made a heavy, liquid gurgling sound while clawing at his throat. Then he lay still.

Kneeling, Hawker turned away and forced himself to inhale deeply, trying to get his wind back. Had anyone heard the hollow thud of the shots? He studied the house closely. There seemed to be no additional lights, no sign of anyone moving inside.

Apparently, they had not heard.

The vigilante made a slow, precise trip around the outside of the house. There was one other guard. He could see the orange bead of his cigarette burning in the darkness of the back entrance, not far from the bank of garage doors. Hawker drew the Randall Attack/Survival knife from its leg scabbard, got down on his belly, and crawled silently across the damp grass. The guard sat on the back stoop, an automatic rifle at his feet. He smoked and stared at the stars. When Hawker was close enough, he lunged from the ground, found the man's throat with his left hand, and drove the Randall through the fibrous wall of his windpipe.

To Hawker's surprise, the guard bolted away from him, running wildly, clawing at his throat and making a harsh gasping sound. Then he sat down abruptly on the asphalt and leaned against the garage. Finally, he keeled over into the blood that pooled beneath him, and died there.

The vigilante cleaned the knife on the grass and studied the house once again. The fury in him was now like a cold, living thing. How would he take them? He thought about it. He wanted to look into their faces; he wanted to see them filled with the same terror they had brought to the lives of so many. He wanted to see terror in the faces of four of them in particular: the three students who had murdered Thy Estes's sister and her family, and Isfahan Shiraz. He wanted to look into their eyes and tell them why they were going to die.

Calmly, Hawker reholstered the knife and slid a fresh clip into the Ingram.

The Iranians' first line of defense was gone now. And their telephone access to the outside world was cut. They were his; each and every one of them was now his.

NINETEEN

The vigilante tested the back door. It was not locked. He stepped into a darkened room of pots and shelves that smelled of grease and curry: the kitchen. As he moved down the hall he swung open each side door he came to: closets; storage areas; then a small meeting area.

The hall opened out into a massive living room. There was a marble fireplace and twin winding stairways. Over the fireplace was a huge oil painting of the Ayatollah Khomeini. A brass display lamp burned above it. In the silent house Hawker carried a chair to the fireplace, stood on it, and removed the painting. Then he braced the painting against the chair at the foot of the stairs. On the mantelpiece he found matches and charcoal starter. He squirted the starter over the portrait, then set it ablaze.

Quickly, then, he ran up the stairs to the second floor. There were darkened halls to his left and right. From his chest-pack Hawker took an Mk 1 illuminating hand grenade, pulled the pin, and tossed it down the stairs into the middle of the living room. It went off with a loud *whoof* and illuminated the entire bottom floor in a searing light.

Suddenly the house was alive. Hawker stepped back into a closet as doors on the second floor began to slam open. He watched silently as more than a half-dozen men, all in pajamas or their underwear, and all carrying handguns, sprinted past and down the stairs. Hawker studied them closely to see if they might be young enough to be college students. He decided none of them were.

At the base of the stairs they stopped one by one, frozen in outrage at what they saw. The face of the Ayatollah was beginning to melt into a gruesome montage of color and flame, all of it illuminated by the garish light of the illuminating grenade. One of the men made a move as if to put the fire out.

"Hey!" The vigilante stood at the top of the stairs, the Ingram held in his left hand, the Colt .44 Magnum in his right. The Iranians all turned toward the voice at once. Hawker smiled at them. "There's only one way I'll let you bastards put out that fire. You can piss on it. Did you hear me? If you want your beloved Ayatollah saved, you're going to have to piss on him."

For a moment Hawker thought a couple of them were actually going to do it. But then they brought their handguns up to fire, which is exactly what the vigilante expected them to do. He dropped to his belly and held the Ingram on full automatic, spraying it like a garden hose. In less than two seconds it was over. Eight Iranians lay at the bottom of the stairs, hands still quivering, mouths open with screams that never made it past their lips. The white marble floor was splattered with red.

From the floor above, Hawker heard the muted thud of someone running. He turned and sprinted up the stairs, reloading the Ingram as he went. As he got to the top of the stairs, he saw an older man disappear into a room and slam the door behind him. Hawker went to the door, jiggled the handle, and stepped back against the wall.

The old man fired through the door four times. The weapon made the substantial *ker-whack* of a heavy-caliber revolver.

Hawker pivoted, kicked the door open, and once again stepped back against the wall.

The old man fired twice more.

Calmly, then, James Hawker stepped into the door, the Ingram held at hip level. "Smith & Wesson, right?" The vigilante's grin was cold. "You're empty, friend."

The man stood behind an ornate bed, cowering against the wall. His hair and pointed beard were gray, and he wore burgundy pajamas. He pointed the gun at Hawker and pulled the trigger three times in rapid succession.

The hammer made an empty clapping sound.

"See?" said Hawker. "What did I tell you?"

The man dropped the gun. "Please," he cried, "please don't kill me. I'll do anything, anything you say, just don't hurt me. I have money, a lot of money. I'll give it all to you—"

"How about just telling me your name for starters."

"Shiraz. Isfahan Shiraz. I am a very important man. If you have already . . . accidentally killed some of my staff, I'm sure a word from me to the police—"

"Isfahan Shiraz," Hawker interrupted, making a friendly,

expansive gesture. "Gosh, I've been looking forward to meeting you."

The old man was immediately wary. "You . . . you have?"

Hawker walked calmly toward him. "Yes, indeed. I've heard a lot about you. Things that might surprise you!" The vigilante's manner became frigid in an instant as he grabbed the man by the collar and banged him against the wall. "I've been looking for you, you sick old son of a bitch, because I want the names of the three students who have been doing your bombing—"

"I don't know what you're talking about—"

Hawker backhanded him across the face. "Don't lie to me, you goat-fucker. You have one chance to live, and one chance only—tell me the names of those students and where I can find them."

Isfahan shuddered, tears rolling down his cheeks. "If I tell you, will you promise . . . promise not to kill me?"

"On my honor."

"You swear it?"

Hawker shook him roughly. "I'm running out of oaths. I gave you my word of honor, didn't I?"

The Iranian began to talk then, too rapidly at first, and Hawker had to make him slow down. He made him repeat everything twice. The students hadn't killed Rultan at the restaurant—one of Isfahan's hit men had because they suspected him of being too friendly with CIA people. But the students had been doing the bombing. When the vigilante was satisfied, he released his grip, smiling. "There, now, was that so hard?"

Isfahan straightened his pajamas, taking a deep breath.

"And let me tell you something else. Because you have spared my life, I swear to you that I will say nothing about your presence here. I will tell the authorities that I do not know who broke into my house. I will swear I did not see the man—the *men*. Yes, the men, who broke in."

Hawker nodded, thinking, *In a pig's eye you won't tell the authorities. You'll tell them everything you can remember about me.* But he said, "That's awfully damn kind of you. Now can I tell you something, Isfahan?"

"Certainly, my friend."

"First of all, sport, I am not your friend. Let's get that straight right from the beginning. Secondly, Isfahan, you can push people like us for a long, long time, and we'll take it. You can take our people hostage, and torture us and screw us every possible way in international business. But do you know what happens when you push just a little bit too hard and go just a little bit too far?"

The Iranian smiled nervously. "No, I do not know."

"I'll tell you what happens," said the vigilante. "We begin to lie like . . . well, like Iranians."

Hawker drew the Colt Magnum, pointed it at the head of Ambassador Isfahan Shiraz, and pulled the trigger . . .

TWENTY

Hawker was awakened the next morning by a discreet tapping on his hotel door that grew progressively louder.

He cracked his eyes and checked his watch.

It was 9:15 A.M.

So much for sleeping late.

"Who is it?"

A familiar voice called through the door, "It's your old friend Lester Rehfuss. Mind if I come in for a minute, Hawk?"

Hawker pulled a pillow over his head. "I don't know any Lester Rehfuss—go away!"

"Now, now, I can always use the passkey if you won't let me in."

Hawker grunted and threw back the sheets. He pulled on a pair of jeans, then swung the door open. Rehfuss stood beaming at him. He wore the same baggy gray suit as when they had first met. In his left hand he carried a leather briefcase. "Good morning!" he exclaimed.

"Don't smile so brightly. It hurts my eyes, damn it." Hawker sat down heavily on the bed and rubbed his face with his hands. "Okay, Lester, this'd better be good. I've been asleep for just about three hours, and I'd really like to sleep for at least another three." Hawker looked at him meaningfully. "If you haven't heard yet, I earned it last night."

The CIA agent sat down on the bed beside him. "I heard, Hawk, I heard. The television people are talking about nothing else. They keep interrupting the regularly scheduled programs to update the nation's citizenry. Really pissed me off this morning. I like to watch the 'Beverly Hillbillies' reruns as I eat my breakfast."

"Please," said Hawker, "you're breaking my heart."

"Don't you want to hear what else you earned—besides our undying gratitude, I mean." Rehfuss swung the briefcase onto the bed and popped open the latches. The briefcase was filled with neat bricks of money that were bound in brown teller's paper.

"A half-million dollars," Rehfuss said just a little wistfully. "Take a closer look at it if you want. It's in small used bills—fifties and twenties, mostly. When the agency makes a seizure of currency, the dough goes into a special slush fund for occasions just like this." He grinned. "I hate to see it wasted on a rich playboy like you, but I have to admit, Hawk, you earned every penny of it. You did one hell of a job."

Hawker looked at him oddly. "I'm flattered, Lester, but I haven't earned anything. Not yet I haven't. I'm not done with this case. I gave the Iranians a pretty hard shot last night, but there are still at least three more members on the loose. They're the same ones who murdered the Chester Rutledge family—in fact, had it not been for them, I wouldn't have broken the case at all. They're students at American University, and they're just about as cold-blooded a trio as you'll ever find. They blew away the whole Rutledge family just because they got mad over some fender-bender auto accident." Hawker shook his head. "You don't owe me one red cent until I deal with those bastards."

The CIA agent stared at him steadily. He motioned at the money without looking at it. "Take it, Hawk. Take the money. You've done a fine job."

Hawker looked at him warily. "Take the money and then go ahead with my plans for the three students?" he asked slowly.

Rehfuss shook his head. "Just take the money, Hawk. Your job is done here."

"But what about the students—"

"Your job is *done*, James," Rehfuss said a little too sharply. Then he shook his head and turned his palms upward in apology. "That's what I've been trying to tell you, James. Your performance last night was phenomenal. I spent the sunrise hours at Isfahan Shiraz's estate—I know. It looks like the Grim Reaper himself made a trip through there. We also found the storage area for the components for the bombs they were using, and enough other evidence to safely conclude that the Iranians were behind the bombings that terrorized Washington, D.C., and killed twenty-seven innocent people. You hit the right people, and you hit them hard enough to knock them out of business for good. We were ready to send in our own team if you failed—"

"You mean you *knew* it was Isfahan's bunch?" Hawker asked incredulously.

"Only after you asked me to check on his name," Rehfuss said quickly. "I said I hadn't heard of Isfahan, but I had. I just wanted to make sure. We had, of course, been compiling data on every diplomat from the Middle East, so it didn't take me long to get a line on him. Within two hours after talking to you, our people had data available on every Iranian in the area who had had public contact with Isfahan within the last six months—and that includes the three students you were talking about."

Hawker nodded slowly. "So the CIA wants them? I can understand that. I don't like it, but I can understand it. The CIA wants its share of the credit, so by arresting the three assholes and charging them with murder—"

"The CIA isn't going to charge them," Rehfuss interrupted uneasily. "Nor is the FBI or the D.C. Police Department."

"*What?*"

"I shouldn't be telling you this, James—"

Hawker leaned toward him, his face red. "Damn it, Lester, you'd better not stop now! What the hell do you mean they're not going to be arrested?"

"Don't get mad at me, Hawk! Hell, I told you what would probably happen if the bombers were caught by the official police. I said they would probably be scolded and deported. If we did anything else, we'd jeopardize the safety of our own foreign diplomats."

"Then why don't you let me go in and finish the job—"

"Because you've had your one chance!" Rehfuss snapped. "We're being blamed for it as it is, but if it happens again, it really is our ass." He leaned toward the vigilante, trying hard to make his case. "James, drop it, for Christ's sake! You've performed beautifully! You've stopped the bastards, and you've left plenty of Iranian corpses in your wake. You made them pay more dearly than any of us ever thought possible. Take my advice, damn it. Take the money, go for a long vacation, and rest assured that, if we ever need you again, we will get in touch."

James Hawker was silent for a long time. "And what happens if I don't drop it?" he asked. "What happens if I go ahead, track down those three slime balls and give them exactly what they deserve?"

Lester Rehfuss's eyes grew serious and he spoke carefully. "James, you once asked me what happened to people who were allowed into CIA's inner sanctum, but later returned to the outside world. It was a legitimate question, and I told you I would tell you when the time was right. Well, the time is right, James, and I'm afraid you're not going to like my answer very much. For you to go against our wishes, for you to turn renegade now, is the same as trying to blackmail us. You may figure that you are safe from disciplinary action because you can always threaten to tell how you were involved with us. But please believe me, James, the organization will not allow itself to be blackmailed. I repeat, it will *not* allow it." Rehfuss looked carefully at Hawker. "Do you understand what I'm saying, James?"

James Hawker nodded. "I understand, Lester."

"I hope you do, James, because if you were to eliminate those three students, you could never stop running. Our people would trail you all over the world. It would not end until . . . until . . ."

"Until I disappeared from the face of the earth, right?" Hawker finished, smiling slightly. He paused for a moment, deep in thought. Then he winked. "That's exactly why I'm going to take your advice and drop it, Lester. Hell, I'm not crazy! I don't want you to sick those Blue Light boys on me!"

The CIA agent grinned with relief. "James, you had me very damn worried for a minute. I thought you were going to get stubborn." He patted the money. "A half-million dollars won't erase your disappointment, but it will go a long way toward *easing* it. Hell, go down to the bar, get drunk. But don't get too drunk. We have a company jet waiting to fly you back to Chicago or Florida, wherever you want to go." Rehfuss glanced around the hotel suite. "I'll send some of our people over to help you pack—say, about noon? They'll do all the crating. You won't have to lift a finger. And I'll notify the pilot you'll be taking off about three this afternoon."

Hawker shook his head. "I know you're anxious to get me out of town, but let's make it later." He smiled rakishly. "There's a certain U.S. senator I want to see. How about if I leave at nine?"

Lester Rehfuss stood up and put out his hand. "The plane will be waiting for you. And thanks, James . . . thanks for everything. It's been a real pleasure to work with you." He clapped the vigilante on the shoulder. "Good luck, my friend."

James Hawker watched him disappear into the hotel elevator. "And good luck to you, too, my friend," he said softly.

TWENTY-ONE

At 7 P.M., just after dark, an auburn-haired stranger confronted Mosul Aski, Zanjen Tabriz, and Karaj Khunsar as they were about to enter their dormitory on the campus of American University. He flipped a badge out at them and quickly returned it to his pocket. He said, "My name is James Hawker. I'm with the CIA."

"Yes?" said Mosul Aski, irritated that the sudden confrontation with the American had startled him. "What do you want from us?"

"I want nothing from you," said the reddish-brown-haired man easily. "I'm sure you heard how some vigilantes shot up Ambassador Shiraz's place last night? Apparently these killers have a real grudge against Iranians. I've been sent to offer you our protection. We're offering it to Iranians all over the city." He shrugged. "But it's strictly up to you. I can stay or I can leave—"

"Oh, stay, *stay*," pleaded the fat Iranian, Karaj Khunsar.

"We are very frightened, are we not, Mosul? You have said so yourself—"

"Silence!" interrupted the young leader. "Are you a baby that you should cry?" He looked at Hawker, saying, "Normally, we would refuse such an offer. We are not children. We can take care of ourselves, and there are few things that we fear." His face filled slightly with contempt. "Unfortunately, in this imperialistic country, you allow madmen to roam the streets, killing innocent Iranians. Because of that, we reluctantly accept your offer of protection."

Hawker nodded. "In that case, I am supposed to transport you to our training station near Fort Stanton Park. You won't need extra clothes or money, and food will be provided by the United States Government."

"But why must we go there?" Mosul asked suspiciously. "Why can't we stay in our dorm and have you stand guard?"

"Because," said Hawker with a touch of impatience, "the people who are killing Iranians don't have much respect for guards. I heard they killed several last night while forcing their way onto the property of Ambassador Shiraz. At the training center, though, there is a complete security system. It's the only place large enough to handle the number of Iranians we expect to arrive—close to a hundred."

"A hundred?" Zanjen smiled. "So many people from the homeland, Mosul, imagine! What a party we will have—and all at the expense of the Americans!"

Mosul Aski continued to stare at Hawker. "Beneath my jacket I am carrying a gun for my protection—a .38 revolver. Will your people allow me to continue to carry it?"

Hawker nodded his head. "Do what you want, Mr. Aski. Actually, I prefer that you hold on to it. It takes some of the heat off me. An extra gun might help if we get caught in a jam."

The Iranian thought for a moment, then nodded his head abruptly. "Good. We will go then! Karaj, Zanjen, come!"

Mosul got into the passenger's seat of the Ford rental car, as Hawker was sure he would—the kid's ego demanded it. The other two Iranians got into the back. As Hawker started the car and pulled out onto the street, he thought, *You stupid bastard, you've played right into my hands. You not only told me that you're carrying a weapon, you told me where you're carrying it. When you die—and you will not die pleasantly—you will curse your own stupidity.*

Hawker drove southwest on Pennsylvania Avenue. He knew it would be the last time he'd see the nation's Capitol as a free man, and he let his eyes linger on the Washington Monument and the stolid dignity of the White House. At Minnesota Avenue he turned north, then drove until he came to a secluded asphalt road fronted by woods and bleak fields. At the first dirt tractor trail beyond a curve, he turned off and stopped the car.

The vigilante had been watching Mosul Aski carefully out of the corner of his eye, and when the Iranian, sensing that something was wrong, reached beneath his jacket, Hawker backhanded him and jerked the little .38 from its shoulder holster.

In his other hand he held the Colt .44 Magnum, which he had hidden under the seat.

"Get out of the car, you scum," he ordered, waving the

weapons at them. "Get out and do exactly as I say, or I'll blow your faces off."

The three Iranian students got out of the car in a horrified daze. The fat student, Karaj, began to sob, then began to bawl out loud. Hawker kicked him in the side. "Keep the noise down, asshole!"

The fat Iranian took one look at Hawker's eyes, then began to gag on his sobs. "He's . . . he's going to kill us, Mosul!" he cried. "Do something, oh, *please* do something!"

Mosul Aski's tough facade had disappeared when Hawker first struck him. The Iranian student held his hands out, as if trying to fend off the inevitable. "You're . . . you're *him*, aren't you? You are the one who killed Isfahan—"

"Right," said the vigilante in a deadly calm voice. "I'm the one who killed Isfahan and his men. And let's not forget that you are the twerps who killed Chester Rutledge, his wife, and three children." Hawker slapped Mosul again, hard. "How many others did you kill, you obnoxious little asshole? Just those four? Or maybe twenty-two other defenseless men, women, and children?"

Hawker's blow had knocked the Iranian to the ground. The vigilante expected him to at least try to fight back, but he didn't. He stretched his hands out toward Hawker in an attitude of prayer, saying, "I will do anything for you. *Anything!* Just spare me, please! I will tell you anything you wish to know!" On his knees, pleading for his life, Mosul Aski also began to cry.

The vigilante looked at the three of them, and he felt neither pity nor triumph. He simply felt sickened by them, sickened by their murderous deeds, and now by their behavior in the face of death. Hawker thought about young Luke Rutledge, alone in a psychiatric ward, living with the horror of his family's death, and he knew he must carry out his careful plan. The punishment of the Iranians had to be equal to their crime, and it also had to say something to the world. It had to tell the world that there were still Americans who could fight back just as viciously as the terrorists who looked upon other Americans as ready prey.

"Take your pants and underwear off," Hawker ordered coldly, pointing the two revolvers at their heads.

"What are you going to do to us?" Mosul demanded to know in a shrill voice.

James Hawker almost smiled. "Nothing you bastards wouldn't do if the circumstances were reversed."

It took him longer than he thought it would to get the three Iranians tied to the tree, gagged and properly wired. Hurrying now, he took the three wires that he had attached to them and bound two of the wires to a stainless-steel ring.

The third wire, the one that was twisted around the small, shrunken scrotum of Karaj Khunsar, the vigilante attached to a bush.

The other side of the stainless-steel ring was already attached to 150 feet of high-tensile-strength airplane cable. Hawker unrolled the cable as he went, then he pulled it across the open road tightly enough so that any car coming around the curve would hit it.

The impact would be so slight and brief that the driver would no doubt continue on, unconcerned.

Of the three Iranians, only Karaj Khunsar, the weakest of them, would survive. Only he would be spared the searing pain and the agony of bleeding to death. But he would live in horror for the rest of his life—just as Luke Rutledge would. More important, though, he would live to return with his story to Iran.

When the cable was set Hawker checked his knots a final time, then got into the rental car and headed back to Washington, where two planes, on separate airfields, waited for him. In one plane Lester Rehfuss would be waiting. Rehfuss would not worry about Hawker's being late at first—after all, hadn't the vigilante already sent his baggage and equipment, along with the briefcase carrying the half-million dollars, to be loaded? Hawker pictured Rehfuss opening the briefcase later and taking the note he had written from among the bricks of money:

Lester: Grant a hunted man a final wish. Take this money and set up a trust for the relatives of the people killed by the Iranians. Also, take whatever funds necessary to make sure Luke Rutledge gets the best care, and the best education, available. Your friend and adversary, Hawk.

Two miles up the asphalt road, Hawker passed a delivery truck speeding inexorably toward the cable he had stretched across the road. He tried to picture the looks of terror on the faces of the Iranians as they heard the first rumble of the truck's approach, imagined the way they would struggle frantically but uselessly as their destiny and death sped ever closer.

How painful would such an end be?

No more horrible than pieces of dead children scattered across suburban lawns . . .

The vigilante shrugged off any thoughts of guilt, and turned his attention to the person who awaited him in the second plane. Because authorities would allow any guest of a VIP to board without question, it was an ideal means of escape for a man now hunted by the CIA. But it would also be a very pleasant means of escape.

But where would they escape to?

Hawker thought about it as he drove. No place in the United States would be safe. How about Little Cayman Island? Or Guatemala—where was there a country more beautiful than Guatemala? Hawker paused for a moment, thinking. What about *Ireland?* His later father would have friends there, and they would take him in, hide him when need be, and he could live pleasantly, flirting with the country girls, exploring the ancient ruins, fishing the fast rivers as they rolled down out of the green hills. It would be pleasant, indeed—until the CIA found him, which it inevitably would.

James Hawker's face brightened as he settled upon his destination. What would it matter to Senator Thy Estes? She had promised to take him anywhere he wanted to go in her government plane.

ABOUT THE AUTHOR

Randy Wayne White was born in Ashland, Ohio, in 1950. Best known for his series featuring retired NSA agent Doc Ford, he has published over twenty crime fiction and nonfiction adventure books. White began writing while working as a fishing guide in Florida, where most of his books are set. His earlier writings include the Hawker series, which he published under the pen name Carl Ramm. White has received several awards for his fiction, and his novels have been featured on the *New York Times* bestseller list. He was a monthly columnist for *Outside* magazine and has contributed to several other publications, as well as lectured throughout the United States and travelled extensively. White currently lives on Pine Island in South Florida, and remains an active member of the community through his involvement with local civic affairs as well as the restaurant Doc Ford's Sanibel Rum Bar and Grill.

THE HAWKER SERIES

FROM OPEN ROAD MEDIA

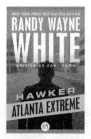
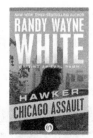

OPEN ROAD
INTEGRATED MEDIA

OPEN ROAD

INTEGRATED MEDIA

Find a full list of our authors and
titles at www.openroadmedia.com

FOLLOW US
@OpenRoadMedia

CPSIA information can be obtained at www.ICGtesting.com
Printed in the USA
BVOW08s1100100616

451539BV00001B/18/P